LISA WEST

The Truth Seeker, The Seer & The Heart

novum pro

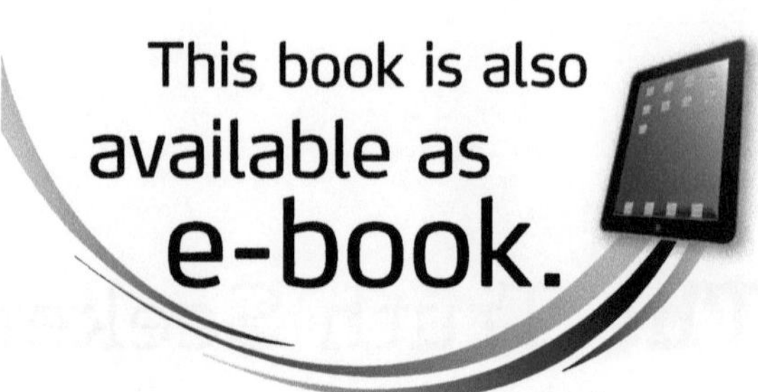

© 2024 novum publishing

ISBN 978-3-99146-504-1
Editing: Vaughn Chambers
Cover photos:
Roma74, Rainprel I Dreamstime.com
Cover design, layout & typesetting:
novum publishing

www.novum-publishing.co.uk

For my hubby, my penguin, my inspiration.

Content

Chapter 1 – Kyle

It was just an ordinary Tuesday. But for Kyle, it would be the day that set the course of his life and started him on a very unusual adventure indeed.

The school hall was unusually quiet. The attention of the entire form was focused on the man taking centre stage at the front of the hall.

Professor Christopher O'Hare was regaling the students with stories of his adventures as an archaeologist. He had a warm, booming voice. Standing at six feet tall, he had bronzed skin from working in the sun and sandy-coloured hair which tended to flop slightly onto his forehead. He had a friendly smile and knew how to tell a story.

He introduced himself by jauntily placing an Indiana Jones-style hat on his head, much to the delight of the students.

He alternately had the children gasping in shock or awe at his stories or laughing at some of the antics of his colleagues. His passion for his work as an archaeologist was contagious, sparking the children's imagination at the wonder of the places he had visited.

Behind him was a white projector screen, which he filled with images of maps of Egypt, and colourful photos of pyramids, temples, sarcophagi, and jewellery made from precious gems.

He told them about the Kings and Queens of Egypt, and how the Egyptians lived and worked, and thrilled them with stories of rituals and magic.

On a table to his right on the stage, he had placed artefacts borrowed from museums and private collectors to show to the children.

Kyle listened with round eyes, straining his neck to see over his school friend in front of him at what might be on the table.

When the professor finished his presentation, he took questions from the students and asked if anyone wanted to look at any of the artefacts he had brought with him. Kyle's arm shot up so fast it was a blur, and he practically bounced in his seat hoping to be chosen. The professor laughed at the number of hands in the air. 'Unfortunately, I only have time to choose a few as I am sure the teachers are hoping to get you back to class sometime this afternoon.'

The professor pointed at a few raised hands, and then he pointed at Kyle. Kyle could not believe he had chosen him; he pointed to himself, and, at the professor's nod, he got out of his chair with a bounce. Bubbling with excitement, he made his way to the front of the hall and up onto the stage. Kyle didn't like to be the centre of attention, so it was noticeably clear how much the talk had interested him. He looked at all the artefacts on the table in wonder. Each piece had a white label underneath with typed information. There were small statues, coins, shards of pottery, and parchment with odd figures on, which the note stated were hieroglyphs.

In a glass-enclosed box, a necklace was shining at him. He had never seen anything like it before. Underneath, the writing said that it was an amulet that had been made to protect the wearer. Kyle didn't know anything about jewellery, but he thought it was beautiful. The centrepiece held a crystal called malachite, which was a stripy green colour. It was encased in what looked like an eye. According to the note, it was the Eye of Horus. This was then surrounded by a flower. The note stated:

'**Malachite** – *Associated with Wisdom & Discernment. Worn to promote prophetic visions and green being a protective colour.*
The Eye of Horus – *Egyptian symbol of protection.*
Flower – **Jasmine** – *For love and protection.*'

The professor noticed Kyle was transfixed by the artefacts, particularly the amulet. The other children had gone back to their seats and the hall was slowly clearing as they made their way to their classes. Kyle hadn't noticed; he was so mesmerised by the amulet. The professor came to a decision. He asked Kyle if he would like to look closer at the amulet. Kyle looked at him with round eyes and nodded. Smiling, the professor passed him a pair of soft white gloves to wear to protect the amulet.

He put gloves on himself, lifted the clear case off the necklace, and removed it from its silk bed. He placed it into Kyle's shaking hands. As Kyle looked at the amulet, he felt a tingling sensation moving up his hands, into his arms, and then through his whole body. As he looked up to question the professor, he felt dizzy. His peripheral vision grew hazy, so he closed his eyes. When the dizziness stopped, he opened them again, but he was no longer in his school hall. The sun was shining brightly in his eyes, and he shielded them with one hand as they adjusted to the unexpected sunlight. As they adjusted, he looked around him. He could see a river to his right with what looked like plants of various sizes and types growing in plots.

To his left, dotted around, he could see houses, although none like he had ever seen before. He blinked and looked up and nearly swore aloud with shock. Before his very, unbelieving, eyes, he was astonished to see a pyramid, just like in the professor's photos. His mouth hung open in complete surprise. He closed his eyes, rubbed them, and looked again.

No, it was not his imagination, as there, in the background, dwarfing the landscape, was a pyramid. It didn't look complete, as if it was still being built. He couldn't help it; this time he did swear. He was interrupted from his swearing by a soft chuckle behind him, and, whirling around, he looked up at the most beautiful woman he had ever seen.

She had kind, brown eyes and long dark hair, and she was wearing strange clothing which looked completely at home in her surroundings. She had a gentleness about her, and he felt as if she could look directly into his soul. He caught his breath as, smiling at him, she reached out for the necklace that he had forgotten he was holding. 'You found it,' she said, smiling. He was passing the necklace to her when he felt the tingling start in his hands again. He wanted to shout, 'NO!' He wasn't ready to leave yet. But before he could do or say anything else, his vision blurred once more. He closed his eyes to combat the dizzy feeling, and when he opened them again, he found himself back in the school hall.

The professor looked questioningly at him, and he found he was slightly out of breath and his head was buzzing. Quite urgently, he thrust the necklace back at the professor. 'You ok lad?' he asked. Was that a gleam in his eye? Did he know what had happened? Before he had a chance to say anything, the bell rang indicating he should be making his way to class. He looked up and realised the hall was nearly empty of students.

'Thank you, sir,' he said, and was about to run off when the professor stopped him and passed him a leaflet on archaeology along with his business card.

'If you have any questions,' he said, indicating the leaflet and possibly the necklace, but Kyle could not be sure. Nodding his head, Kyle ran down the aisle out of the hall. He stopped off in the bathroom and splashed water on his face. Feeling less dizzy, he made his way to class.

He could barely concentrate for the rest of the day in school. So many thoughts and questions were going through his head. *Had he really been in Egypt, or had he been daydreaming? Who was the beautiful woman and what was her connection to the amulet?* So many questions. He looked up and noticed Mr Thompson looking at him questioningly. Realising he had been caught staring into space, he returned his attention to his textbook and tried to concentrate on his schoolwork.

He knew one thing for certain. He wanted to be an archaeologist when he grew up. He wanted to know who the woman was that he had seen. He ... just wanted to know.

He could not wait to get home from school that day. As soon as the last bell of the day rang, he grabbed his bag and ran out of the door. Waving goodbye to his mates, he cycled home as quickly as he could.

When he made it home, he abandoned his bike on the drive and opened the door, leaving it wide open. Then, thinking better of it, he turned around and banged the door shut. Dropping his school bag on the floor, he discarded his coat and shoes in the middle of the hallway where anyone could fall over them. Calling 'Mum!' at the top of his voice, he ran down the short hallway into the kitchen, where he found not only his mum but also his dad. It was unusual for his dad to be home at this time of day, being a salesman, but he had a long-distance journey tomorrow, so he had come home early in preparation. Kyle had obviously caught his mum and dad kissing but chose not to notice, as he was too excited to tell them about his day to stop and effect his usual retching motion at the view of them kissing.

He told them very excitedly about the professor who had visited the school. He told them about how he was an archaeologist, had brought cool stuff for them to look at, and told them some amazing stories of his adventures. 'He was like Indiana Jones,' Kyle said to his parents. He told them about the cool necklace, and that he knew that he wanted to be an archaeologist when he grew up. Then, leaving them both startled, he ran out of the room. He ran back in to ask for a snack, grabbed his bag from the hallway, leaving his coat and shoes still in the middle of the floor, and then ran up the stairs to his bedroom which he shared with his older brother.

He emptied his pockets of their contents, rubber bands, marbles, and tissues, onto his dresser and was surprised to see what looked like sand in the palm of his hand. He carefully tipped the sand from his hand into a discarded, but empty, sandwich bag to keep.

Back in the kitchen, his mum and dad looked at each other in the wake of his whirlwind entrance and exit and smiled. Thinking that by next week he would probably want to be a footballer or astronaut, they thought nothing more of it.

Chapter 2 – Amira

'Amira?' Amira turned at the pressure of a hand on her shoulder. Dragging her eyes away from the spot where the boy had been standing just a moment ago, she looked into the concerned eyes of her husband Abubakar.

'Who were you talking to?' he asked gently.

'A boy,' said Amira. 'He was standing just there.' She gestured with her hand which was holding the amulet.

'Where did you find it?' said Abubakar.

'The boy brought it to me,' said Amira. 'He was wearing the strangest clothes and shoes. He had pale skin and the most startling blue eyes. He gave me my amulet and then he just disappeared.'

'Do you think he was a vision?' asked Abubakar.

Amira shook her head. 'A vision wouldn't have been able to give me this,' she said, refastening the necklace around her neck. 'I think the amulet brought him to me.'

'I wonder why,' said Abubakar.

'I don't know,' said Amira. 'But I have a feeling we will meet again.'

Abubakar gently took Amira's hand, and they walked back into the house.

Chapter 3 – Emma

Chione woke up with a start, her heart pounding in her chest. Something had disturbed her, but she wasn't sure what. Listening carefully in the darkness, she heard it again. With a start she realised it was their daughter Emma. She shook her husband Matthew awake and they quickly got out of bed.

Putting on her dressing gown, she hurriedly left the room, with Matthew close behind. She made her way along the corridor to Emma's bedroom and turned around to Matthew with concern on her face only to find that he wasn't there.

She went into Emma's room and heard him enter behind her. She turned to him confused. Understanding her unasked question, he waved his phone at her. Emma was having another nightmare and was crying out in a language they didn't recognise. 'Brother, wake up, brother, Baahir, wake up please you are frightening me, please, please wake up.'

Chione went to comfort her, but Matthew put a hand on her shoulder to stop her. She looked up at him in confusion and he placed his fingers to her lips to silence her. Using his phone, he started to record what Emma was saying.

It only took a few minutes, but listening to Emma in obvious distress and not doing anything was breaking her heart. Thinking enough was enough, she looked at Matthew, and with a gentle smile, he nodded his head, just as distressed. Chione went to Emma who was thrashing around in her bed and gently cradled her in her arms. 'Emma, Emma, wake up sweetie, it's ok, it's only a dream, mommy and daddy are here.'

Emma cried out again, 'I will go for help,' she shouted.

'Shhhhh Em, shhhhh now, it's ok, I have you, you are safe.' Chione gently rocked her until she relaxed in her arms. Emma eventually quietened and fell back into a restful sleep. Chione and Matthew watched her for a little while and then quietly left the room and made their way to the kitchen. Matthew put the kettle on, and they sat at the kitchen table.

'I wonder what she was saying. She sounded so distressed.'

Matthew glanced over at her from the kitchen counter while he waited for the kettle to boil. 'I don't know,' he said. 'At least we have a recording now. Perhaps we can finally find out.'

'It could be Arabic,' Chione said. 'It sounds a little bit like how grandma spoke when I was little, and we visited her. It has been so long since I have heard it spoken, I am not sure.'

Matthew placed a steaming cup of tea in front of Chione; she wrapped her hands around it, comforted by the heat. He sat down with his tea and replayed the recording on his phone.

'I will speak to Mark our linguistic expert at the museum when I go to work tomorrow. Hopefully, he can shed some light,' said Chione.

'Good idea,' said Matthew. 'Come on love, let's take our tea to bed.'

Chione gave him a watery smile, 'Let's just check on Emma first.'

They walked hand in hand to Emma's room and were glad to find her sleeping deeply and restfully. They both kissed her gently on the forehead and made their way back to the kitchen to get their tea. They settled back into bed and, after a while, with Chione in his arms, Matthew tried to go back to sleep. They could not help but listen out in case Emma woke up again but finally fell asleep themselves.

Yawning, Chione woke up the next morning determined to find Mark when she got to work to see if she could find out what it was Emma was so frightened of.

Emma came into the kitchen looking sleepy but unaffected by her nightmare the night before. 'Good morning sleepy head.'

Emma gave her a sleepy kiss on the cheek. 'I had a funny dream last night,' she said.

'Did you?' said Chione. 'Can you remember what it was about?'

'It's a bit blurry,' said Emma, 'but I think it was about a boy. He was hurt. He had hit his head on a rock, and I couldn't wake him up. Then you and Daddy came into the room, and I don't remember any more.'

'That's ok Emma, sweetie. Nothing to worry about. It was just a dream.' Smiling, she gave her daughter a hug and made her some breakfast.

Later, Chione picked Emma up from school and they walked home. 'Did you have a nice day at school sweetie?' asked Chione.

'Yes Mommy,' said Emma. 'I painted a picture for you,' she said, passing Chione a picture she had painted in art that day.

The picture was of a little girl planting some seeds in a vegetable patch. 'Thank you,' she said, smiling at her daughter. 'Who is this of? Is it a friend at school?'

'No Mommy,' giggled Emma, 'It's Amira. You know Amira Mommy?'

'Amira? That's an unusual name. Is it a new girl in the street?' Emma hadn't heard her as she was happily skipping ahead towards home. Chione was sure she had heard the name before, but she just couldn't remember where. She racked her brain trying to think of all the families in the street and whether any of their daughters were called Amira, but she couldn't recall.

Shrugging her shoulders, she caught up with Emma and walked the rest of the way home. She helped Emma with her homework at the kitchen table and then started to prepare dinner. Chione then remembered Emma's imaginary friend. She had walked in on Emma many times talking to someone she couldn't see. She even spoke in what Chione had thought was a made-up language, but after Emma's nightmare when she had shouted out in the same language, she had researched it by asking Mark at work and found it was a form of Arabic.

'Have you told me about Amira before?' Chione asked Emma. At Emma's nod, she said, 'Is Amira your home friend? The friend you play in your room with sometimes?' Emma nodded again. 'Can you tell me about her?'

Emma thought for a moment, scrunching up her face in concentration. 'She is from far away where it is hot and dusty. She wears funny clothing,' she said, giggling. 'But she thinks I wear funny clothes. She plants seeds to grow food. She is very smart and knows the names of lots of plants. She says she helps her daddy grow them. She has long dark hair and wears funny white clothes.' Emma lost interest in the topic and went back to her drawing at the kitchen table. Chione decided to leave it for now and went back to cooking, but she decided to pay more attention when her daughter was playing in her room.

Chapter 4 – Amira

Amira woke up with a start, her heart pounding. *It was just a dream*, she told herself. But she knew that wasn't true. She knew the difference by now, no matter how young she still was, between a dream, or even a nightmare, and one of her visions.

She heard raised voices and her mother crying in the other room. She shot out of her bed to listen to what was going on.

It turns out her brother had snuck out to see his friends in the middle of the night. This wasn't unusual, but it was now mid-morning, and he hadn't come home yet.

It was not the safest place to be out at night and she could tell that her parents were worried. She knew she had to tell them her vision but hated the looks on their faces and wariness around her when her dreams come true.

She had seen her brother hurt and knew he needed help. Taking a deep breath, she walked into the living room and spoke. 'Mother, Father, I know where Baahir is.' Her parents looked at her with confusion, her mother with tears in her eyes, but they didn't say anything.

She saw understanding dawn on Anipe's face and, wiping her eyes, she gestured for Amira to come over to her. Amira walked across the room and her mother took the shawl from her shoulders and wrapped it around Amira. It wasn't until then that Amira realised that she was shaking. Her visions always had that effect on her. She would wake shaking, feeling slightly sick and breathing heavily as if she had just been running.

Her mother rubbed her arms to warm and calm her and then sat her on her knee, cradling her in her arms. 'Tell me what you saw,' Anipe said gently. Amira thought back on her dream. She recognised the place that she had seen Baahir lying. It was somewhere they had played before and somewhere she had followed him and his friends to when they snuck out.

It wasn't far and she described the setting and directions as best she could to her parents. She thought that Baahir had been on his way home along the Nile bank and slipped. He had hit his head on a rock and knocked himself out. She had seen blood near the bottom of his head but remembered him still breathing. It was cold out and she felt they needed to hurry. Amira wanted to take her parents to him, but her father, Baniti, wouldn't allow it. He recognised the setting that Amira had described and felt he would be able to find Baahir on his own.

Baniti left quickly with a blanket and cloths, and salve to tend to the wound Amira had described seeing, leaving Amira and Anipe waiting anxiously.

Anipe was keeping lookout at the window and saw Baniti approaching. She opened the door and Baniti walked through with Baahir in his arms. Baahir was obviously still unconscious, and Baniti looked worried.

Baniti lay Baahir on the bed and Anipe removed his damp clothes and dressed him in clean, warm clothes. Baniti slipped out of the door to fetch their neighbour Ramla, the local healer. Anipe put some water on the fire to boil to help Ramla tend to Baahir's wounds. Ramla came quickly, although it was clear she had been woken up. Baniti walked over to Anipe and gave her hand a reassuring squeeze which was met with a watery smile. Ramla had a basket with her; when she lifted the cover, Amira could see that it was filled with strips of clean cloth, pots, and bottles of ointments, salves, and herbs. She unwrapped the bandage that Baniti had fashioned around Baahir's head to staunch the blood.

When she had removed it, they were relieved so see that the bleeding had slowed down and almost stopped. The water was ready and Ramla asked Anipe to fill two bowls with it. Anipe brought over the warm water and Ramla first washed her hands in one of the bowls and dried them on a towel that Anipe passed her. She then added a liquid from one of the many bottles in her basket to the other bowl. She cleaned the wound with a clean cloth and, after applying some of the salve, re-dressed the wound.

Amira watched in fascination as Ramla worked with skilled efficiency, but also gentleness. The fact that Amira had watched everything she had done hadn't escaped Ramla's attention. She filed that information away for a later date and vowed to speak to Anipe when she next had her alone. Ramla took a small pouch out of her basket and filled it with a selection of herbs which she gave to Anipe with instructions to put them in water for Baahir to drink when he woke up.

She left confirming she would come back in a few hours to check on him, and if he stirred before then, to come and fetch her. Anipe hugged her friend with gratitude. She told her that she would bring her vegetable soup and freshly baked bread for her and her family's supper as her payment and thanks. Amira could see that Ramla would have liked to refuse, but it was their way. The small village looked out for each other and always respected the gifts that each could share.

Anipe was also a fine cook, so how could anyone say no to her food. Ramla smiled and said she looked forward to it and that her mouth was already watering at the thought. She left quietly and Amira sat by Baahir's bed to watch him and held his hand gently.

Anipe cleaned up and sat on the other side of Baahir and did the same. They looked at each other across the bed with understanding and, bowing their heads, they shared a prayer that Baahir would wake soon and that he would be well again.

Amira had fallen asleep in the chair, slumped over slightly onto the bed. A groan and then a gentle squeeze of her hand woke her from her slumber. She looked up and rubbed the sleep from her eyes. She was delighted to see her brother's eyes open. 'Baahir,' Anipe said, kissing his hand. Baahir tried to lift his head off the pillow and, with a groan, let it fall back down again. 'Slowly,' Anipe said.

'My head hurts Mother,' said Baahir. 'What happened?'

'You fell and hit your head,' said their mother. 'You have been unconscious for a while. You had us worried. I'll get you something to help.' Their mother filled a cup with water and stirred in the herbs that Ramla had left them.

Lifting Baahir gently into a sitting position, she placed the cup to his lips. 'Drink slowly,' she said, 'It may be bitter, but you need to drink it all. It will help.' Baahir took a sip and screwed up his face. He tried to push the cup away, but Anipe was insistent. 'Drink it all son, it will help.' Baahir did as he was told, at times trying not to retch but managing to drink it all down. Anipe then brought him fresh water to drink, which he drank in great gulps despite being told to drink slowly. Seeing that this had tired him, she settled him gently onto the pillow. At Anipe's nod, Amira left to let Ramla know that Baahir was awake.

Ramla came with her basket again and checked Baahir's pulse. She also asked him to follow her finger with his eyes, and satisfied with what she found, she said he could sleep again for a while and that she would be back to check on him in an hour and re-dress his wound. Baahir slept and let the herbs do their work.

Ramla checked Baahir's wound again later that day and decided he needed some stitches, of which he tried to protest loudly. She hushed him and said that once she put her salve on his wound, he wouldn't feel a thing. He looked dubious but let her. Anipe held his hand through the whole thing and Amira was amazed to see that he didn't even flinch when the needle entered his flesh. Again, Amira watched fascinated and didn't feel squeamish at all at the sight of the needle piercing flesh just as it would a piece of material.

Ramla checked on Baahir over the next few days, cleaning his wound and checking his stitches as well as his pulse, temperature, and eyesight. She asked Baahir questions such as his name and age, and his mother and father's names. She asked him if he had a headache and double vision. She seemed happy with his replies and each time left herbs for Baahir to drink to help with headaches and potential fever. Baahir turned green at the mention of the herbs but, seeing how they helped his head to stop hurting, grudgingly swallowed the bitter potion.

After watching Ramla for a few days, Amira asked her what she was checking for, and Ramla gently explained she was checking for infections and whether the knock to the head had left any after-effects to Baahir's brain.

Ramla checked on Baahir over the next few days and was happy that he could leave his bed for gentle walks to check his balance. Pleased with the results, she allowed him to increase his walks until he seemed like his old self. He was to keep his cut dry and to keep applying the salve that she gave him. After about seven weeks she was happy that the wound had healed and removed the stitches. Baahir soon returned to good health and went about his days as normal.

Baniti and Anipe never told him about Amira's dream and that it was because of her that he was found and saved. Anipe knew he would ridicule Amira over it and wouldn't be grateful. Amira was relieved and the matter was soon forgotten.

Chapter 5 – Amira

Amira grew up in Tara, which was one of the few villages remaining in Egypt. The land was fed by the Nile River, its lifeblood, making the earth very fertile. As Egypt evolved, villages slowly disappeared making way for bigger towns and cities. Amira's father Baniti inherited his land from his father and when their neighbours had moved to already populated bigger towns, Baniti bought their land.

As farming evolved, Baniti evolved his land and crops too. He irrigated his land so that it was rare that he was affected by droughts. Over the years their farm grew in size and their land provided food for their table in the form of vegetables, fruits, and herbs. Later it brought money as they sold the produce that they grew at the local market. They also transported crates to the neighbouring areas by boat, depending on the amount of crop they had produced that year.

When Khnurn, his wife Femi, and son Abubakar arrived in their village, Baniti and Khnurn decided to join forces. Baniti lost some of his profits due to the cost of shipping from their village to the surrounding towns and Khnurn imported the goods that he sold. They felt that it would benefit them both to join forces, and soon Baniti would own his very own ship which he called *Egyptian Swift*.

Baniti kept experimenting with his land and Khnurn was always bringing him seeds and cuttings from far and wide. He would also bring news of any innovations as they happened, and thanks to their joint venture, they were able to sell produce to towns further afield. They made good business partners and became loyal friends.

Amira helped her father Baniti with the harvest and her mother Anipe to prepare meals, and as she grew older, her father would sometimes take her on the merchant ships, which always felt like an adventure.

Amira started to help her parents on the market stall too selling their produce. The markets were always loud and bustling with merchants calling their wares. The air would always be thick with smells of herbs and spices and her eyes would grow round in wonder at the sight of beautiful silks and precious gems.

She had begun to understand that her prophetic dreams were considered a gift to many in Egypt. Her mother worried for her safety and, mostly, kept her gift quiet to protect her. Anipe called them her *special dreams*. She always knew by Amira's face in the mornings if she had had one of these special dreams and would ask her to tell her about it. If the dream was about someone they knew, she would have a quiet word and they would just drop by, unexpectedly of course, the next day. Anipe would ask Amira to tell them what she had seen. They would always leave an offering of whatever they could manage. Vegetables or herbs for the dinner table, pieces of cloth, grains, or spices, and even seeds for planting. Anipe would always refuse, but they always managed to forget to take their offering with them.

Anipe worried that word would spread of Amira's gift, but their village was a close-knit community and very protective of each other. Sometimes these dreams were happy messages, such as a long-awaited baby, or helped someone find something precious they had lost. However, sometimes they were sad, and Amira always left it up to Anipe whether the person was to be told or not. If it were a death for instance and telling them wouldn't change anything but just cause distress, she didn't want to worry them sooner. Sometimes it was a hard decision to make. Sometimes Amira's dreams were of an accident on one of the merchant vessels or in the market. Anipe always kept an eye out when attending their market stall and if she were able to intervene, she would.

One night, Amira dreamt that she was at the market, and she saw a display of masonry jugs collapse and a small child passing at the time was crushed under the load and badly hurt. Two days later Anipe was at the market tending the stall and saw a precariously packed stall of masonry jugs. She politely offered to help the old man who ran the store to restack them, so they were safer. He thanked her profusely. His son normally stacked the stall but was unable to be there that day to help. With his arthritic hands, he found it quite difficult on his own. So, they both hoped that this was one incident they had managed to prevent.

Other incidents were out of their hands and Anipe tried to teach Amira to let these go as she couldn't stop everything, but she could see the toll that they took on Amira. Anipe always held Amira when she cried at the injustice of seeing what she could not help to prevent.

Ramla had noticed Amira's interest in the work that she did and offered to teach her about herbs and how to make potions so that she could help people. Amira learnt so much from Ramla over the years. She taught her about herbs and flowers and how to use them for healing, whether as tinctures, potions, balms, or antiseptics, both topical and taken in food or water. She taught her crystal therapy and how to use the gemstones topically or as essences. Not only that, but she also helped Amira to hone her gift of sight.

It was usual for a girl of twelve to be married, but Amira wasn't ready and instead agreed to be a student in herbal medicine, working with Ramla, who was one of their town's priestesses. As this had been her wish from the moment, she had watched Ramla look after her brother when he was hurt, Amira was very happy with how things turned out.

Working with Ramla, Amira found that she could have waking dreams when holding something personal from the person being read for or about. She found that these were generated from a strong emotion. Readings like this tended to leave her energy drained and Ramla helped her regain this with one of her potions. They decided, though, that she would only do these types of readings in emergencies.

When Baahir turned fourteen, he split his time between the farm and working aboard a ship delivering merchandise to towns along the Nile River. Amira stayed with her mother to work on the farm and to produce her healing potions.

Once she had gained knowledge and was confident in her herbology, people started to visit her at home to barter for potions for various maladies, even for finding love and mending a broken heart. She also sold them on their market stall and her father started to add them to his crates to be shipped to the surrounding towns. This brought in a good income and Amira was happy to help her mother and father have a better life. When Baniti and Khnurn joined forces and their business venture grew, they made sure that Amira kept her money, which she hid carefully for her future or put towards anything she wanted to buy. Her first gift was for her mother. She found some beautiful silk at the market and made her a scarf. Anipe loved that scarf and said it made her feel beautiful.

Amira soon had repeat customers who had ailing health and bartered for her potions. They would purchase these from her father and then he would deliver the potion to them the next time he was in their town.

At the age of fourteen, much to Amira's delight, Baniti allowed her to accompany him and her brother Baahir to some of the local towns where she could sell her herbs and potions in person. She dried and hung her own herbs and sold them like this after discussing ailments with the clientele. She also sold her potions and balms. Her father set her up a little tent at the end of their stall so she could talk in private with her customers. Most of her customers were women and she would also offer crystal healing to some of her clients. She was always selective and got a feeling from her customers before she offered this treatment.

On one of these excursions, she was resting in her tent having completed a treatment when the flap was pulled back and the most stunning women Amira had ever seen walked in. She was dressed in beautiful garments of silk. Her long dark hair was shiny, and she had the most startling green eyes surrounded by charcoal eyeliner.

She asked Amira's name and, after confirmation, nodded her head and entered the tent fully. She didn't give her name, but Amira could see that she was a lady of standing. She had the most beautiful necklace around her neck with turquoise and lapis lazuli. 'My friend advised me to seek your help. She promised that she would let me know when you were back in the area so that I could come to visit.' She took a deep breath. 'My husband and I desperately want a child you see. Sadly, I miscarried at the beginning of last year and haven't been able to conceive since.' The lady had a cultured voice and Amira could see the sadness in her. 'My husband has paid for the best doctors, and I have been poked and prodded, and followed all their instructions, but to no avail. I fear I am unable to give my husband a child. Our marriage didn't start as a love match but to align our families' wealth. We quickly fell in love and thought children would come in time. We are now under a lot of pressure to produce an heir as my husband's father is in poor health and wants to see a grandchild before it is too late.'

As Amira looked closer at the lady, she could see the sorrow and the strain of the situation in her face, under the carefully applied makeup. The lady held herself very regally with her spine straight and her hands gently cupped in front of her. 'I don't know if you can help me,' she said. 'I think that my husband would probably laugh at me being here. No offence, but he would wonder what you could offer over the best physicians in the country. My nurse was a healer and I have much respect for her and for her knowledge. It was her that recommended you. Do you think you can help?' the lady finished in a rush.

'Would you like to sit?' said Amira, gesturing to the silk padded cushion on the floor. She smiled apologetically as she didn't have a chair to offer her. The lady gracefully sank onto the cushion in front of Amira and, as if all her poise had left her, she broke into noisy sobs. Amira took her hand gently until she was able to control herself once more.

'That is a good start towards healing,' she said gently. 'Holding all that in does not help.' The lady smiled a watery smile at Amira and then opened a purse that she carried with her and restored her appearance.

When she had regained her poise, she once again looked Amira in the eye. 'I feel lighter,' she said, with a slight smile. She looked like she wanted to apologise for her lack of control, but Amira sensed that she wasn't sure how to begin. Amira felt that she wasn't a person who had to apologise for herself in life.

Amira gently nodded her head to acknowledge what the lady was unable to express. The lady seemed to relax slightly and nodded back. 'Do you have something I could hold? Something that you wear often and means a lot to you. If you have something of your husband's as well, that would be useful.'

The lady had come prepared it seemed. She first took the necklace from around her neck. 'This was my husband's grandmothers, and he gave this to me when he proposed. I have worn it every day since.' She then opened her bag and took out a ring. It was quite chunky, and judging from the size, it belonged to a man. 'This is my husband's; it was given to him on our wedding day. It also belonged to his grandfather. This is the first time he has taken it off. He thinks I am getting it cleaned for him.' She then handed it to Amira.

Amira prepared herself as Ramla had taught her. First, she lit a candle to bring in the light. She sat cross-legged on her own cushion with her hands gently cupped in her lap. Taking some relaxing breaths, she closed her eyes and imagined a root growing from the base of her spine gently anchoring her into the ground. She imagined earth energy drawing up the root into her spine, flowing through her body and out of the top of her head, disappearing into the sky, going further and further until it joined the gods themselves. She then imagined energy coming back from the gods, creating her connection to their healing. This travelled back down through the top of her head, back through her body, and through her root back into the earth, thereby creating a bridge between the earth and the gods.

This took about five minutes. The lady watched her intently during the process. Amira opened her eyes. Taking more cleansing and relaxing breaths, she then lit a bundle of sage and swirled this around her head and torso to clear her aura. After getting permission, she did the same to her client. Prepared, she sat cross-legged once more and gently took the necklace and ring the lady had brought with her.

Closing her eyes, she focused on the energy coming from the items that she held. There were many emotions coming from both items, but Amira tuned into a particular event which had brought the lady to her today. At first, she was assaulted by the great emotion coming from both items at the loss of their baby. Amira could feel the love from the husband for his wife and the support he had offered her in overcoming such unbearable loss. Amira felt tears flowing down her face. She did nothing to stop them or open her eyes to wipe her face but kept attuned to her task.

Ramla had taught her to protect herself to an extent while using her gift so that she didn't get drained by others taking her energy without realising it. However, they had both concluded that she couldn't shut herself off completely as this also hindered the vision, so she let some emotion flow freely. Images started to flash in front of Amira's eyes like a dream, but she was awake. She saw one doctor after the other visit the lady.

She saw the lady following their advice and the subsequent tears when, once a month, it was clear that the treatments hadn't worked.

She felt the despair growing and the hope dwindling after every doctor and as time went on without her conceiving. Amira felt all this and then she let it go, like studying a leaf and then dropping it in the river and watching it float away. She left the past behind, letting other images come and go. She then saw images of the lady before her with child looking healthy and happy. She saw her give birth to a healthy baby boy and then, two years later, to a healthy baby girl.

The gods also showed her images of the lady herself. They showed her a darkness in the lady's aura and the husband's aura centring around their reproductive organs. Amira was satisfied that with the healing she could provide, the lady would conceive within six months. Satisfied that she had been given all the information she required, the images stopped. Amira opened her eyes and gave the lady back the necklace and ring. The lady refastened the necklace around her neck and placed the ring back in her bag.

She looked at Amira expectantly. Amira told the lady she would like to scan her and give her some crystal healing. The lady gave permission and, picking up a large quartz wand, Amira gently scanned the lady's aura, noticing the changes in energy and blocks around the lady's heart and her reproductive organs. She placed crystals around the lady on the floor in a circle for grounding and, using the clear quartz like a laser, she went around touching each crystal connecting them in an invisible circle. She then pointed the quartz towards the lady and moved down the front of her body slowly as if she were drawing an invisible line in the air. She did the same behind the lady and then focused the point on the lady's heart and then abdomen. She did this three times in total, drawing the line front and back, then focusing on the heart front and back, and then the abdomen front and back. Afterwards, with her hands, she stroked the air a few inches from the top of the lady's head and over the front of her body to her feet. She did the same over her back and then removed all the crystals.

She gave the lady some water and a black tourmaline crystal to help her ground so that she wouldn't be dizzy when she stood. She watched the lady closely and, when she finished the water, nodded at her satisfied that she would be ready to leave soon. Amira then made a potion of hilba and Egyptian honey to aid fertility. She selected a moonstone from her crystals. 'I want you to place the crystal in water in the moonlight overnight and for you and your husband to drink the water each morning. You need to do this for a week.

I want you to come back to see me for two more treatments in the next two months.' The lady agreed and advised that she would be informed when Amira was next in their town.

She then told the lady what she had seen in her vision. There was such hope in the lady's eyes. She paid Amira generously and, taking the potion and crystals, promised to follow her directions and that she would see her next month.

The lady turned up the next month, confirming that she had been following Amira's instructions. 'I told my husband of my visit with you,' she said sheepishly. 'I thought he would laugh, but he just smiled gently and said he would drink the water with me. He asked if he should come with me for my last visit. Maybe have a treatment himself.' Amira agreed this would be a good idea and on the next visit did a joint healing on both the husband and wife which she felt was the most powerful yet. The lady and her husband left holding hands.

Five months later, Amira was walking with Abubakar back to her father's ship. Abubakar had been escorting her back to the ship for the last three months and she loved his company. Amira heard her name called, turned around, and saw a familiar lady walking hurriedly towards her. She reached Amira out of breath. 'I thought I would miss you. I came to thank you and to give you this.' She handed Amira a parcel. Amira took it and looking from the parcel to the beaming lady, she remembered where she had seen her before. She looked from the lady's smiling face down to where her hand rested on her gently rounded abdomen.

'Congratulations,' said Amira.

'It is because of you,' said the lady. 'I am truly grateful for your help.'

'You are very welcome my lady,' said Amira.

'Please, my friends call me Khepri.'

'Khepri,' said Amira. Recognising the great honour bestowed on her, she blushed and nodded her head. 'How are you feeling?'

Khepri smiled. 'Good,' she said. 'The sickness stopped last week, and I have a lot of energy,' she paused, 'for my husband,' and blushed. Amira, realising what she meant, blushed also.

'When the time comes, if you have any problems, although I don't foresee any,' she said quickly, not wanting to alarm the lady, 'I will give you the name of a healer. She lives in my town and is a priestess at our temple. She is a great healer who taught me. She would want me to give you her name.' Amira passed Khepri a parchment of paper with Ramla's name on it and the name of their town. 'My father's ship is *Egyptian Swift*, and they are here every week. He would be able to get a message to Ramla should you request it.'

Amira was unsure what to do next and Khepri looked at the parcel that she held clutched to her chest. Glancing at Abubakar who had stepped slightly away to give them some privacy, she smiled knowingly at Amira. 'It will make a beautiful wedding dress,' said Khepri. Amira glanced at Khepri in surprise and then followed her gaze to Abubakar. Sensing their gaze, Abubakar looked up and smiled at Amira. Khepri was not insulted by his slight. She knew love when she saw it. Amira looked back at Khepri blushing.

'We are not betrothed.'

Khepri smiled knowingly. 'You will be,' she said. Laughing at Amira's face, she said, 'You don't have to have the sight to see that. His love for you is clear.' Khepri clasped Amira's hands in hers nearly dislodging the parcel onto the floor. 'Good luck my friend and thank you for helping me give my husband this wonderful gift.' Smiling, with tears in her eyes, Amira bade Khepri goodbye.

She walked up to Abubakar who gallantly held out his arm for her to take. She looked into his eyes, praying that Khepri was right and that he did love her as much as she did him.

Chapter 6 – Baahir

Although Baahir was loved and cared for equally with Amira, he grew up spoilt and selfish. From a young age he always seemed to want what everybody else had. He could have the same dinner as his sister but hers always looked nicer or he was convinced that she had more than him. His parents tried to reassure him that this was not the case, but he never listened. Without realising it, they gave in to him more than they should have to keep the peace and so did Amira.

When Amira was six and Baahir was eight their parents gave them both a piece of land to grow whatever they wanted on. Amira followed the advice of their father Baniti on how to tend her plot and started with vegetables and grains that her father advised would grow well in the soil. Her plot grew and prospered, and she supplied many crops for the dinner table. Baahir on the other hand had no interest in farming and didn't listen to his father's advice; he planted what he wanted in a half-hearted attempt. He was jealous when Amira's did well and believed that their parents had given her the better plot and that was why her vegetables grew well while his withered and died or didn't sprout at all.

What Baahir didn't take into consideration was that, while he was off playing with his friends or causing trouble at the market for the merchants, Amira was tending her plot. She spent time working with her father to correctly irrigate the plot from the river, feeding the soil, and nurturing the roots to grow. She took time to weed and trim and remove pests from the plants and vegetables. She followed Baniti's advice on what to plant and when to harvest the plants so that they would still bear fruit and veg.

Baahir failed to accept that Amira got a good harvest because of the work she put in and that he hadn't because of his lack of care. Sadly, as he got older, he became lazier and his belief that the world owed him a favour grew.

Abubakar loved Amira at first site, meeting her through her brother Baahir who he befriended when they first moved to Tara. Their friendship grew more out of proximity than like. He would spend time with Baahir playing by the Nile River or running through the markets full of merchants selling their wares.

Amira was a small slip of a girl with long dark, almost black, hair flowing freely down her back, and the darkest pool of brown eyes he had ever seen. He could see that she was gentle and kind. In her eyes was a wisdom and knowing beyond her years. Not that he recognised this as a child, but more so as they grew into adolescence and adulthood. When she looked into his eyes, he felt as if she could see right to his very soul. She must have liked whatever she saw because she would always smile at him after.

As time went by, she grew into a beautiful and gentle young woman, and he fell more deeply in love with her each year.

Baahir grew into a handsome man but didn't have Amira's kindness of spirit and became more discontented with life the older he got. For some reason that only he knew, he always acted like life owed him in some way. Nothing was good enough for him. He always wanted more or thought he deserved more.

Abubakar was always careful not to show Baahir how he felt about his sister, for fear that he would use her or him in some way to get what he wanted. He feared that he hadn't hid his feelings well enough and, as they grew older, he tried to distance himself from her, even though it hurt to do so.

Sadly, Baahir had noticed and felt that Abubakar's feelings for Amira would be useful to him in the future.

The one skill Baahir cultivated was his observations. He knew which merchant undercut another; he knew what people needed and used his time on his trips with his father to make contacts with traders from other towns. He listened and he provided what people were lacking, whether it was grain for flour as the crops hadn't grown that year or a particular fabric for a *gentleman* to give his mistress. He also knew people's secrets and prided himself on missing nothing. Unfortunately, he was quite happy to use this knowledge for his own gain.

Chapter 7 – The Knights of Ramla

The Knights of Ramla was formed to protect time travellers and to hide any evidence of their travel.

The group was currently run by Bay Isson, who was a descendent of Abayumi Isson, the son of Amira and Abubakar. A scientist, he had grown up with stories passed down through his ancestors about Amira and her Truth Seeker. Later, when he turned twenty-one, he was presented to The Knights of Ramla to carry on the family tradition.

The archives were full of stories and artefacts much like those of Amira and Abubakar. Initiation into The Knights was generally through bloodlines, but sometimes others were invited, from all walks of life, with their own stories to tell and their own gifts to contribute. It was an honour to become part of The Knights and Bay hoped to live up to the expectations of his father and their ancestors.

He was assigned to Kyle and Emma as their story was interwoven with Amira and Abubakar's. Due to their connection to his ancestors, it was only right that he would be their guardian on their journey. Instructions had been left and he knew when the time came that the amulet would make its way to Kyle.

During his time at university, Bay had met a young Italian woman called Francesca. Francesca was everything he wasn't, and he was smitten at first sight. Where he was studious and had his future planned out, Francesca was an art and dance major. She was free spirited and wanted to follow life where it took her. Unfortunately for Bay, when they graduated from university, life took her to Paris, where she wanted to express herself through her art. At the time he was heartbroken and vowed he would never love another woman like he loved his Francesca.

Francesca was into complementary therapies and was always trying out new treatments such as reiki, crystal therapy, and reflexology. She would sometimes drag him to Mind, Body, and

Soul events where she would buy crystals and incense, have holistic treatments, or see a psychic for a Tarot reading.

Bay didn't put much stock by it himself but went because he knew how much Francesca enjoyed going. Seeing his scepticism, Francesca tried to get him to see the science behind the treatments. At her urging, he sat through workshops on reiki and crystal therapy, and he read up on reflexology and acupuncture.

During one of their visits to a Mind, Body, and Soul event, Francesca talked him into having his aura photographed. Intrigued by the colours around him in the photograph and the explanation of what emotions they represented, he asked Francesca to explain the principle of the aura to him. It was interesting how each of the complementary therapies interconnected and how they worked with the body and mind.

Smiling with excitement, Francesca lent him some books to read. At the next event they attended, Bay noticed the same aura photographer as before. He asked him if he was willing to come to the university with his equipment and meet a friend of his who was an engineering student. The photographer agreed and they met the following week in the science lab at lunchtime and he explained to them both how the camera worked.

He told them that the receptors in the metal plates where you place your palms measure the electromagnetic field by monitoring acupressure points that correspond to Ayurvedic meridians, which are energy channels in the body. An attached data box then converts the energy readings into frequencies that correspond to certain colours.

Alongside his academic studies, Bay continued to research the electromagnetic field as well as meridians and colour therapy, not realising at the time how useful this information would be once he joined The Knights.

Michael also joined The Knights, and with the help of volunteers who claimed to have time travelled, he gathered data. Bay borrowed the artefacts that had aided their time travel and conducted his research. From this research, with the help of Michael, he built a machine and wrote a programme which

monitored the electromagnetic field of each person and artefact. He found that the electromagnetic field of the artefact
mirrored the electromagnetic field of the person they were connected with. He also found that the vibrations of the artefacts
changed and pulsed when close to the person. It was as if the
artefact knew they were there.

Bay used this research to build and create a prototype sensor
to place with the artefact to monitor its electromagnetic field.
He decided he would start with his ancestor Amira's amulet as
an experiment. So, he placed a sensor in the box of the amulet
and waited for it to make its move.

One day the amulet started to emit a different frequency
and Bay knew its time was near. His friend and fellow member
of The Knights, Christopher, had received an invitation to tour
universities across the midlands. He was to talk about his recent
book and his archaeological adventures. He hoped this would
inspire the next generation of archaeologists.

He asked Bay if he could include the amulet among the artefacts to take with him. Bay felt it was the right time and agreed.
He placed a program on his friend's computer so that they could
monitor the amulet on his journeys.

After a few weeks, Christopher advised Bay that his tour had
gone well, although it had now come to an end and there had
been no readings emitted from the amulet of any note.

Bay was disappointed. He felt that it was time, but there was
nothing more he could do. Christopher was due to stay with an
old college friend in Coventry for a few days to relax after his
tour. He wished him well and said he would see him when he
got back.

Christopher was relaxing with Greg laughing over old school
escapades. 'I have a favour to ask you,' said Greg.

'Ask away,' said Christopher.

'I wondered if you would mind signing your book for David?'
Christopher had met Greg's son David earlier that evening and
found out he was studying Egypt in history at school and was
loving it.

'Of course I wouldn't mind,' said Christopher.

'Do you know what?' said Greg. 'He would be made up if you talked at his school before you left.' Feeling he may have asked too much, he added, 'Only if you want to. I know you came here for a break. No pressure my friend,' holding up his hands and then pouring them another drink and changing the subject back to their school days. They were soon shaking with raucous laughter with Christopher threatening to tell David about some of the trouble Greg had gotten them into.

Christopher spent some of the next day discussing his book with David and showing him photos of artefacts he had found on his many expeditions. He regaled him with stories of his adventures and David sat with huge eyes. Greg laughed saying he had never seen him so quiet.

'You have a way of telling a story my friend. I feel like I was there with you,' he chuckled.

When Christopher was closing his files down on his computer, something made him check the software that Bay had put on it to monitor the amulet. To his amazement, the graph was spiking all over the place. He wasn't entirely sure what this meant, so he called Bay to let him know.

'Has anything unusual happened over the last couple of days?' Bay asked. Christopher filled him in on his last few days but couldn't pinpoint anything that would have alerted the amulet.

'My friend's son isn't called Kyle so it can't be him,' Christopher mused aloud. 'Maybe the school?'

'Yes, yes,' said Bay, 'that must be it. You must visit that school. Take a few more days off before you come back to make up for it. Go to that school, it could be really important.'

So, the following Tuesday he found himself standing at the front of a hall full of children at Chamberlaine High. He was used to speaking to university students and felt a little nervous. His talk went well, and near the end, he decided to ask some students if they would like to come up on stage to look closer at some of the artefacts he had brought with him. He was gratified to see so many hands go up so fast. He picked a few children and held his breath.

As they made their way up to the stage area, Christopher went over to his computer and set the thermal imaging program that Bay had installed so that he could not only monitor the frequencies omitted from the amulet but also from the children around it. It also showed changing images of the energy field of the amulet and the auras of the children within the imaging field. He watched as each child moved within the field range to see if there was any change. Nothing, until one boy stepped in front of the table. He was reading the cards beneath the artefacts and looked genuinely interested. When he came to the amulet, his eyes grew round, and he stood still like a statue. Christopher watched the changing colours on the screen as the boy was transfixed by the sight of the amulet. What was also astonishing was that the colours of the energy around the amulet matched his as they changed.

With excitement, Christopher knew this had to be the boy they were waiting for. The other children were trailing off by now, leaving the boy behind. The boy didn't notice, so mesmerised was he by the sight of the amulet. It was as if it was reaching out for him. He approached the boy. 'Would you like to take a closer look?' he said, pointing to the amulet. The boy looked at him with round eyes and nodded his head.

After he had passed him the amulet, he stepped back to observe the boy who he now was sure was Kyle. The boy had grown very still as if he was in a trance and had closed his eyes. It was only for a short time and then Kyle opened his eyes and was blinking as if dazed. Kyle thrust the necklace back at him. 'You ok lad?' asked Christopher, concerned.

Kyle opened his mouth to speak but before he had a chance to say anything, the bell rang. The hall was nearly empty of students and Christopher felt his time running out.

'Thank you, sir,' said Kyle, and was about to run off. Christopher stopped him and passed him a leaflet on archaeology along with his business card.

'If you have any questions,' he said, indicating the leaflet and necklace, not sure how much to reveal. Nodding his head, Kyle ran down the aisle out of the hall.

Christopher worriedly watched Kyle leave the hall. He had looked pale and shaky. He hoped he would be ok. He walked back to the computer and was surprised to notice that his own legs felt shaky. The boy had gone so still as he held the amulet and it had been a strange sight to behold. He rewound the footage on the computer to see the images it had recorded. Bay would analyse all the data, but he was intrigued what the visual images would show. He didn't understand it all completely as this was Bay's baby; he would ask him to explain fully once he got back. He sent Bay all the data straight away as he knew their importance to his friend.

He split the screen so that he could see images of the boy, who he now knew to be Kyle, and the amulet side by side. The most astonishing thing happened. The colours on both screens fluctuated and changed until it seemed that they synchronised with each other. Then, in the moment when the boy went still as a statue, the colours stopped altogether as if there was no energy coming from the boy or the amulet. As if he was just a shell and nothing more. The essence of Kyle, the energy of him, had gone. Christopher blinked a couple of times.

Smiling, he wished his friend was standing by his side; he would have slapped him on the back. *Well done my friend*, he thought. He would take him a bottle of Jack Daniels to celebrate. It seemed that his friend had done what he had set out to do. Bay had created a software that could monitor time travel. Christopher knew he had been working on it for some time and he could see the proof before his eyes, because, although the physical form didn't seem to go anywhere, it was obvious from the readings and the images recorded in front of him that the person's energy did. It also proved that the frequency of the artefact was part of the time travel process. Shaking his head in wonder, Christopher turned off the computer and packed up his things ready to go.

Chapter 8 – The Knights of Ramla

Christopher made his way to The Knights' headquarters at his earliest opportunity. He was eager to see Bay and find out what he thought of the readings that he had sent him. He absentmindedly greeted his colleagues while making his way to Bay's office. Frustratingly, he wasn't there. He walked back out and saw Kevin in the corridor. 'Hi Kevin, mate, do you know where Bay is?'

'He is in the lab,' he said, indicating over his shoulder.

Christopher thanked him and made his way down the corridor to the laboratory. Bay was standing in front of a bank of monitors, each filled with data and images. Bay looked up at the sound of Christopher's entrance. 'Well done my friend,' said Christopher, slapping Bay on the back and presenting him with the bottle of Jack Daniels that he had purchased just for the occasion. 'Come on, open it up, we have some celebrating to do.' Laughing, Bay opened the bottle, and getting two cups from the drink's dispenser, he poured a healthy measure in each cup. He took his first sip savouring the flavour and heat as it smoothly covered his tongue and throat and heated his belly.

'So, what do you think?' said Christopher, indicating the computer monitors.

'It's astonishing,' said Bay. 'It performed better than I ever could have imagined. You can even see the exact moment when Kyle travels. The data I have are amazing. It's as if the artefact connects with the person on a molecular level, as if it chooses the person.'

'You do realise you are going to have to go bigger with this don't you?' At Bay's quizzical look, he carried on. 'You have found a way to monitor an active artefact. You need to create a more mobile model that we can each carry on our person. Like a watch, to activate and alert us to a possible active artefact. We need to build it into museum security systems so that we can monitor larger areas. Just imagine what we could find,' he said, looking

at the monitors and then his friend and colleague with awe at
what he had created. 'I'm impressed my friend and that doesn't
happen often.' He saluted him with his cup.

Bay looked from his friend to the monitor, his mind buzzing with possibilities. 'I would need to put a specialist team together,' he mused aloud.

'Kevin would be a good place to start,' said Christopher. 'He
has abilities yet untapped when it comes to technology and security systems.' Bay agreed. They sat down to savour the rest
of their drink and talked about other people they could recruit
into the team from their colleagues.

Chapter 9 – Kyle

It took Kyle a whole week to build up the courage to go to the school library. He waited until there was only ten minutes left of lunch and, leaving his friends playing football, snuck off while they were occupied.

Reaching the library with heart pounding and hands shaking, he pushed open the library door and stuck his head inside. The library looked empty. He knew the librarian Mrs Daniels would be somewhere because the door was open, and she always locked it when the library was empty.

It was so quiet in the library. All he could hear was his shoes squeaking on the floor. Nervously, he looked around and then jumped onto the carpeted area so he would not make a noise. Looking at the signs on top of the shelves, he located the history section and started to scan the books on the shelf. He spotted a book on archaeology and gently pulled it out. Opening the book with shining eyes, he flicked through the pages and marvelled at the brightly coloured pictures.

With his heart pounding, he made his way to the counter where he found Mrs Daniels watching him, a smile on her face. He smiled back and asked to check the book out.

Mrs Daniels had seen Kyle come into the library and thought she would keep an eye on him, just in case his friends had sent him to cause mischief. She watched him jump onto the carpet because his shoes were squeaking on the floor of the walkway and tried not to laugh. She had never seen him in the library before, although she had seen him around school. Cheeky and boisterous, just as a boy should be in her opinion, though he was polite too. She watched him pull a book from the shelf and flick through it. She thought he would just put it back on the shelf and leave, but to her surprise, he started walking to the counter.

She smiled at him hoping to make him feel less nervous, and then he gave her a cheeky, slightly cocky, smile. She thought,

This boy will break hearts one day. I bet when he smiles like that, he could probably be forgiven anything. He handed over the book to be checked out, but when she handed it back to him, he looked uncertain of what to do. Understanding, she asked him if he would like to come back after last class and collect it. He would then be able to put it in his bag and take it home. Relieved, he smiled back at her and nodded his head. With a little wave, he ran hell for leather out of the library, no longer caring that his shoes made a noise and hoping to get out of the library unseen by any of his friends to avoid the risk of being teased.

Just a couple of weeks later, he turned up in the library early before class and pulled the book out of his bag and passed it back to her. 'Would you like another?' she asked. He nodded and, dumping his bag onto the floor, he ran to the shelves. Scanning them quickly, he pulled one from the shelf, ran back, and, smiling, passed the book over. She scanned it, another on archaeology she noticed, and he stashed it in his bag.

This became a routine. Every couple of weeks he would return one book and take another until he had exhausted their collection. When he told his mum that he had borrowed all the school had, she got him a library card for Coventry Library and, for Christmas, he had a subscription to an archaeology magazine. His mum, seeing his interest was not waning in any way, also signed him up to the YAC, the Young Archaeologists' Club, where he could participate in practical sessions.

Kyle studied hard at school, and for extracurricular activities, he would be with the YAC. He soaked everything up he could and knew this was still what he wanted to do. He was advised to complete A-levels in history, English literature, geography, geology, and biology, which he stayed on to complete at Chamberlaine High.

When it came to university, he applied to Cambridge, not knowing how he was going to be able to pay. Amazingly, he was accepted, and with his acceptance letter, he was notified that he had been given a scholarship to pay for his attendance.

Chapter 10 – The Knights of Ramla

The team that Bay and Christopher had put together had been working on the software project for months and were making good progress.

'My only concern in making it more widespread is security,' said Bay.

'Are you worried someone might use it for nefarious reasons?' asked Kevin.

'Do you believe in God, Kevin?' At Kevin's shrug, Bay continued. 'I'm not sure either but I have seen a lot since doing this job and heard a lot from stories from my father. I know from science that the universe needs balance. People like Emma and Kyle are effectively changing history. We are aware of people like them, and we seek to protect them and the artefacts, but others might see it as meddling in the bigger picture. Because of time travellers like them, people who were meant to die survived. Maybe they created a whole line of descendants that wouldn't have existed before. On the other hand, what if these people weren't meant to die in the first place? What if it wasn't their time to die and they only died at other humans' hands? Maybe the universe is trying to create balance by using the artefacts to change their fates or even recorrect them.'

'Wow! This is way too philosophical for me,' said Kevin. 'You've been giving this a lot of thought, haven't you?' he said, trying to lighten the mood. 'OK, we need a beer if we are going to be putting the world to rights. We have been at this for weeks. We need some down time. I know a place. How about a beer and pool?'

'Sounds good but you are buying,' joked Bay.

Kevin mulled this over.

'OK, but you are paying for the takeaway.'

'Deal,' said Bay, chuckling.

They tidied everything away and secured the premises before heading out. Kevin watched his friend. He looked like he had the weight of the world on his shoulders. 'I appreciate Christopher's enthusiasm, but let's take things slow. Okay? Right, enough shoptalk.'

Kevin got the drinks in and set up the pool table. He knew the owner of The Rabbit & Hare as they were old army buddies. He always got privacy here, so it was a great place to unwind and decompress.

'Do you mind if I ask one more serious question? Then that is it, I promise,' said Bay, holding his hands up in surrender.

Kevin looked at his friend. 'Sure, but then be prepared to get thrashed,' he said, indicating the pool table.

Smiling, Bay appreciated his levity. Kevin nodded his head, indicating he was listening. 'What I said earlier. Do you think I was talking a load of rubbish?'

Kevin was tempted to make another joke, but he could see that his answer was important to his friend. Kevin sighed, 'No, I don't. I'm not saying I understand all of what we do, but I know that there is more to life than we know. I think the fewer people who know about our project the better, and however we proceed, we proceed with caution. This will need to have some damn good protection so that no one can detect it, hack it, or copy it. Luckily for you, you have me,' he said, giving Bay a cocky grin.

'Like I said, I appreciate Christopher's enthusiasm, but we may need to rein him in a little.'

Begrudgingly, Bay nodded his head. 'Let's all meet up to hash this out.' Bay pointed to the table. 'After you.'

Kevin was true to his word and thrashed Bay in the first game, but Bay got his revenge and thrashed him in the second game. Debating between playing a decider or food, their growling stomachs made the choice for them, which was probably for the best as the pub was filling fast, and others wanted to use the table. Being competitive men, it was possible to play all night, with neither wishing to concede.

Neither of them felt like eating back at the office so they decided on an Italian restaurant. The waiter took their orders and poured them both a glass of wine. 'Cheers!' Clinking glasses, they savoured their first taste of the wine.

'So, how is the family? said Bay.

'Good,' said Kevin. 'Izzy is taking advantage of the twins starting school and has applied to teach computer science and artificial intelligence part-time at the university. She should hear any day now. 'What about you? How are Zoe and Sarah?'

'Good,' said Bay. 'Zoe is shattered but is looking forward to getting back to art restoration when Sarah starts nursery next month. Life is good my friend.'

'I'll drink to that,' said Kevin, and they clinked glasses once more. The waiter brought their food and the conversation turned to sport as they enjoyed their meals.

Chapter 11 – Emma and Kyle

Kyle first met Emma through an online archaeology forum at university, which they had been encouraged to join to connect with other students from around the world to share insights and knowledge. It grew to become an international study group and support network for all involved.

Kyle connected with Emma straight away and they became fast friends. Emma was studying at California State University, San Bernardino. She was studying applied archaeology as well as linguistics and anthropology.

She was smart and funny, and it wasn't long before they were chatting over *Google Duo* with pizza and beer. She gave him an alternative perspective on many subjects, and they had lively debates. The loser, they decided, would pay for the next takeaway. They always finished their debates as friends and sometimes with tears of laughter and aching sides.

Emma's mother worked at Rosicrucian Egyptian Museum, San Jose, California, which had one of the best Egyptian exhibits in America. They were always having collections on loan from private collectors, which would fill a special display created for this purpose. Emma would send him literature and photos before they became live on the museum website, and he jokingly called her his 'woman on the inside.' She loved Cadbury chocolate, and he teasingly sent her some as a bribe for this information.

He slowly fell in love with her, and she felt the same way, but after a long discussion and with some sadness, due to the distance they lived, they decided for now they would remain friends, as neither of them wanted to lose the other's friendship. Who knew what the future held?

They both knew if things had been different that they would have been more than friends.

They found that they both supported American football, although different teams. So, when The New England Patriots or Los Angeles Rams were playing, at a time that suited them both, they would watch together connecting with *Google Duo*. It almost felt as if they were in the same room as each other.

Emma introduced him to her mom and dad, Chione, and Matthew. Her mother had Egyptian origins and Emma explained her name meant *mythical Nile daughter*, while her dad was Californian born. Kyle could see instantly that Emma resembled her dad. Her mom was small and delicate-looking with exotic chocolate-brown eyes and long black sleek-looking hair. Her father was tall and stocky. Emma told him that her dad had been a quarterback at high school, which Kyle could have guessed given his build. He had sandy brown hair, and green eyes that twinkled and crinkled at the corners when he smiled. It was obviously from her dad that Emma had gained her passion for American football. From her mom came her love of history and archaeology. He wouldn't find out till later where her interest in linguistics came from.

She also got her passion for cooking from her mom and surfboarding and climbing from her dad. It was obvious from watching them together that they all had a close bond and loved and respected each other. He liked them instantly and, thankfully, they felt the same way about him.

Kyle also introduced Emma to his parents and three brothers. His mum loved to read and cook. She had worked in retail for most her life, but when he had gone to university, she decided to turn her love of reading into a career and studied to be a proofreader. She now worked part-time at King Publishing and got to read the latest upcoming writers' work before others.

His dad had a passion for sport which he also shared with Kyle and his three brothers. He decided to put his journalism degree, so far unexplored, as well has his love of sport and uncanny ability to say the exact same words just before the commentator, which left his family looking at him with open mouths and him laughing, to good use and left his sales job and became a sports commentator.

Chapter 12 – Amira

When her father cast off *Egyptian Swift*, Amira settled in for the voyage. Normally when she was aboard, she would be standing watching the views go by as she loved to see the bustling villages, new buildings and temples being built, and plants and wildlife along the banks of the Nile. She loved all the sounds and smells, but in this instance, she was distracted by the package in her lap given to her by Khepri.

She gently untied the ribbon holding the material together. As the material parted, it revealed the most beautiful white silk. She lifted the material gently and her breath caught as it seemed to shimmer with rainbow colours as it picked up the light. *It would indeed*, as Khepri had said, *make a beautiful wedding dress*, she thought, blushing.

In the middle of the fabric was a pouch. Intrigued, Amira picked up the pouch, and opening the top, she looked inside. With eyes as round as saucers, she emptied a handful of gemstones into her palm. Eyes glowing, she marvelled at how much such gems must be worth. One of the gemstones caught her eye above the others. It had stripes of light and dark green with swirling patterns across its surface. She remembered from her teachings with Ramla that this was malachite, a protective stone. It would absorb negative energies and help attune her spiritual guidance. The other gemstones were a mix of lapis lazuli, turquoise, amethyst, chalcedony, feldspar, garnet, jasper, obsidian, olivine, and quartz.

Amira marvelled at Khepri's generosity and wondered if she should give the gifts back. She remembered the joy on Khepri's face and the great gift she had helped give her with aid of the gods and decided it would be rude to return the gift so generously given. She felt that Khepri had given the gift with great joy in her heart. Amira looked around her to see if anyone was watching. As much as she trusted her father's men, she couldn't

be too sure. She safely tucked the pouch inside the hidden pocket of her dress, wrapped the beautiful fabric back up, and put
it in her satchel to keep it safe. She couldn't wait to show her
mother, Anipe, later.

Chapter 13 – Amira and Abubakar

On her sixteenth birthday Abubakar invited Amira to join him for the day. He had a delivery to make, and he was going to visit his friend to see the garden that he had created.

Amira was excited to be able to spend a full day with Abubakar, and after getting permission from her parents, she agreed. They made an early start, and the weather was beautiful. Amira stood watching land and houses sail by, enjoying the refreshing wind on her face, even if it was blowing her hair into a tangle. She laughed aloud with delight, drawing the attention of Abubakar and quite a few of his crew. At Abubakar's glare, they diverted their eyes back to their work, but not without a smirk in his direction.

When they disembarked, Abubakar left his crew to unload the goods, and taking Amira's hand in his, he lifted a basket in the other and led her into the throng of people making their way to the market. Stopping at one of the stalls, he bought Amira a bouquet of jasmine flowers, her favourite. 'Happy Birthday Amira,' he said.

Blushing, Amira took the small bouquet and inhaled their gentle fragrance. 'They are beautiful, thank you Abubakar.'

'Not as beautiful as you Amira,' he said, and lifted her hand to his lips for a gentle kiss.

Amira felt tingles radiate up her arm from Abubakar's kiss. A gentle flush travelled through her body and her heart beat faster. *I love you,* she wanted to say aloud but felt too shy. They began to mill through the crowd once more, stopping at stalls to talk to people they knew or to admire the merchandise. Amira had never felt so happy, so free, and at the same time, so safe. Holding Abubakar's hand, she felt as if she could fly. She felt herself stand up straighter and felt confidence flow through her. She felt more herself than she had ever felt. The pride showed on Abubakar's face when he introduced her to his friends. The tender smile he sent in her direction made her heart swell.

They made their way through the market and Abubakar led her down a narrow street away from the noise. They came to a pretty little courtyard with several gates leading off. Abubakar led her to one of the gates and, opening it, led her inside. The sight that met her eyes made her gasp aloud. It was a walled garden. All around the outside were small trees and vines heavy with fruit. In the centre was a small pond with lilies floating on the top. There were pots of flowers of every colour she could think of, and the air was fragrant with their blossoms.

In the centre of the pond was a small fountain, and to one side was a marble bench in the shape of a half circle. Abubakar placed the basket on the bench and led Amira around the path so that she could take a closer look at the garden. 'It's beautiful,' she said. 'So peaceful. Who created this?'

'My friend,' said Abubakar with pride. 'He has created larger scale gardens at two of the palaces, but this one is his pride and joy because it is his.' Abubakar led Amira to the back of the garden where there was another gate. They walked through and Abubakar knocked on the door on the other side. A small woman holding a gurgling baby in her arms opened the door.

'Abubakar,' she said, smiling. Abubakar kissed her on the cheek.

'Tifi, this is Amira. Amira, this is Tifi, Saju's wife, and this little one is Sinu.' Sinu gave Amira a toothy grin and Amira smiled back.

'He is adorable.'

'Thank you,' said Tifi. 'It is lovely to meet you Amira, please come in. Can I get you a drink?' Tifi led them both inside as Saju came out of one of the rooms off the hallway. Abubakar and Saju greeted each other with claps on backs and Abubakar led him over to Amira.

'This must be your Amira,' said Saju, his smile broadening. After a quick glance at Abubakar at the term *your*, she smiled at Saju.

'Your garden is beautiful. As is your home,' said Amira.

'Thank you,' both Tifi and Saju said at the same time, making them all laugh and dispelling any tension in the air.

Saju put his arm around his wife's shoulder. 'I hope you don't mind but we just have to pop out on an errand,' said Saju.

At his wife's confused glance, he squeezed her arm gently. 'Yes,' said Tifi.

'We shouldn't be long though. Please enjoy the garden while we are gone,' said Saju.

'See you both in a while,' said Abubakar and he led Amira back into the garden. Amira politely smiled, a little confused, but followed Abubakar.

Abubakar took the basket off the bench and they both sat down, absorbing the tranquillity of the garden. Abubakar lifted the cover off the basket and Amira could see that he had brought a picnic for them. She was touched by his thoughtfulness and gently kissed him on the cheek to say thank you. He placed a cloth on the bench between them and laid out the fair of cheese, bread, and fruit. He had even brought some wine with him, which he poured into two small cups. 'Happy Birthday Amira.'

'Thank you Abubakar. This is all wonderful. Thank you. I can't remember a birthday which has been this special.' Amira felt tears of wonder in her eyes. He made her feel so special.

Relaxing in the garden, they enjoyed their food and easy conversation. She always felt so relaxed with Abubakar; she could talk about anything and ask him any questions that she wanted. He never shushed her like her brother did or tried to make her feel silly. He always listened to her and gave her his full attention. She would cherish this day always. She glanced around her trying to commit every detail to memory. The way the light fell on the flowers and the water in the pond. The sounds of insects buzzing around the flowers and the water trickling from the fountain, and Abubakar's handsome face smiling at her.

She closed her eyes trying to connect with each sound. When she opened them, Abubakar was looking at her intently. He was so handsome. Her Abubakar, because no matter what happened, in her heart he would always be her Abubakar. The thought of him marrying someone else nearly broke her heart.

'I have a gift for you,' he said, and turned to reach for his satchel.

'More?' said Amira. 'What more could you possibly give me? You have already given me so much.'

'I would give you the world if I could,' said Abubakar. 'I want to give you everything in my power to give, and so much more.'

Give me your love, thought Amira. *That's all I truly want.* But she couldn't say it out loud. She didn't want to spoil the day. She didn't want it to feel awkward.

Abubakar took out something wrapped in cloth and passed it to Amira. 'This comes with a question,' said Abubakar. 'And my pledge to you.' With a beating heart, Amira gently opened the cloth to reveal a beautiful amulet on the end of a delicate chain. In the centre of the amulet was the malachite that Khepri had given her. She would have recognised the pattern anywhere, as each gemstone was unique. She had given it to Abubakar to look after for her as she was concerned that her brother would find her hiding place and take it to sell.

It was set into the Eye of Horus on top of a jasmine flower delicately carved from precious metal. It was beautiful and Amira looked at Abubakar with eyes shining with love. Abubakar went down on one knee in front of her; he took the necklace from her shaking hands and placed it around her neck. 'Perfect,' he said.

'You know, whenever I smell jasmine, I think of you,' said Abubakar as he took Amira's hand. 'I have loved you from the first day we moved into the house next door. You smiled at me shyly and my heart knew. Amira, this gift is my pledge to you. I love you, heart, body, and soul. You are beautiful inside and out, and if you do me the honour of being my wife, I promise to protect you with my heart, body, and soul for my whole life and even after.'

In his other hand he held a delicate band with a small rose quartz crystal at the top. He looked at her with such love in his eyes that Amira felt her heart was ready to burst. 'Abubakar,

I would be honoured to be your wife. You are the best man I know. I accept your heart and promise to keep it with mine always.' Abubakar gently placed the ring on her ring finger. He then kissed her, pouring out all his love in that kiss, stealing her breath and sealing his pledge.

Chapter 14 – Amira

Amira carefully removed the wicker basket from its hiding place in the floor of her bedroom. It had been created specially to fit into the space. Her hiding place had used to be the space in her bed pallet, but a few years ago she had gone to use some of the money she had saved for a project she was working on and found that all the money had gone. Money, she had saved over many years towards her future. She had been devastated. Even more so when she realised who had taken it. She had told her mother Anipe straight away and Anipe looked stricken. 'Who could have done this?' said Amira. As they looked at each other, they both knew in their hearts that there was only one person it could have been.

'I will speak to your father when he gets home, and we will both speak to Baahir. He has been spending a lot of money on that girl he has been seeing, but he told your father that he made a bit extra on a deal he conducted recently. He seemed to be trying harder, so I guess we wanted to believe him.' Anipe was wringing her hands. 'How much is missing?'

'All of it,' said Amira, and she broke down sobbing. She had saved carefully, and the possible betrayal of her own brother had broken her heart.

Anipe comforted Amira, and when she had settled, they discussed creating a new hiding place. Both her father and brother were working away until later that night, so they knew they were alone. They carefully dug a hole in a dark corner of Amira's room where any difference in the floor would be hard to see. They covered the inside as best they could to stop the damp penetrating. Anipe then fashioned a wicker basket to place inside to hold any of Amira's treasured items, but nothing ever felt safe again. Anything truly precious she decided to ask Abubakar to look after for her. He was honourable and she trusted him to take care of any possessions or money for her.

Later that night when Baahir and their father Baniti arrived home, Anipe took Baniti aside to tell him about the missing money. Baniti turned to look from Amira's stricken face to the face of their son. Baahir instantly looked concerned, and his eyes kept straying to the door. 'Amira's savings have gone missing son. Do you know anything of this?'

A fleeting look of guilt passed over Baahir's face, but he masked it quickly. 'Why would I know anything?' he said, but his voice wobbled slightly.

'Did you take the money Baahir? And don't bother trying to lie to me,' said Baniti, anger deepening his voice. 'Because I have learnt to see through your lies. When you started spending money you didn't have, I wanted to believe you when you said you had acquired it through work. In my heart I knew you were lying. From Amira, Baahir … from your own sister. I will not have theft under my own roof. Did … You … Take … The … Money?' said Baniti with controlled anger. 'Think very carefully before you answer.'

Baniti was a strong and proud man who worked hard for his family to give them everything he could. He couldn't abide lazy people and didn't tolerate them in business. The men that worked for him recognised this and they also recognised that he paid a fair wage for a good day's work. They respected him and were loyal. They found it hard to believe that Baahir was his son as he was lazy and had no pride in anything that he did. They found him sly and devious and not to be trusted. They were always polite to him for Baniti, but they didn't respect him.

Baniti was a big man and not quick to temper, but he wasn't afraid to stand up for himself or what he believed. He stared Baahir down now; he had tolerated enough and would not let this pass. He wanted an answer, and no one was leaving this house until he had gotten to the bottom of where Amira's money was. Baahir began to squirm under his father's steady gaze. He tried to look belligerently back like he didn't care what his father thought, but the cracks were starting to show. He looked to his mother and sister but could see there was no help in those quarters.

He looked his father in the eye, squared his shoulders, and spat out, 'Yes.' He waited for his father to rant at him, but Baniti continued to level his gaze on him and lifted one single eyebrow, which had a wealth of meaning. The silence became uncomfortable.

'Why?' said Baniti.

'Cara said she was going to finish with me and find someone who could take her places and buy her things. What was *she* going to do with it?' He sneered in Amira's direction. Amira had never realised before the disdain that Baahir seemed to hold for her. 'She doesn't go anywhere, do anything. What is she saving it for anyway? Her marriage? Who's going to marry someone like you.' He sneered again, looking directly at Amira now. Amira lost her temper for the first time in her life. Baahir was twice her size and all she could see was that cruel sneer on his face. She walked up to him and before she could think better of it, she swung her fist with all her might and punched him right in the face.

Baahir was unprepared and swayed on his feet. He brought his hand up to his bloody nose. He started towards Amira sputtering, 'You B...!'

'I suggest you don't finish that sentence,' said Baniti. 'Is there any money left?' he asked. Baahir shook his head, careful of jostling his nose which was starting to drip blood through his hand. Seeing he wasn't going to get any help from Anipe who seemed stunned into silence, he ripped some cloth from his shirt and tried to staunch the blood.

Baniti stood still. With controlled fury, he didn't take his eyes off Baahir. Underneath the fury was sadness and resignation. He looked from Baahir to Amira and Anipe and back to Baahir. It was his place to protect his family. The fact that they had been hurt from within angered and saddened him. He couldn't let Baahir stay. Anipe and Amira were his priority now. 'I suggest you collect your things from your room and leave.' His level stare was back on Baahir now. 'It has been time for a while that you made your way in the world.'

Baahir walked to his room and his father followed. 'Making sure I only take what is mine?' he sneered at his father. But there was fear under the words. He wished he could take it all back, everything he had said, but he couldn't apologise. It just wasn't in his nature. So, he would brazen it out and pretend that he didn't care.

Baniti just stood in the doorway watching. When Baahir had collected everything, they walked back into the living space. His mother couldn't look him in the eye, and he couldn't bring himself to look at Amira. He had seen her face when he had slung his spiteful words at her. He hadn't meant any of them, not really. He had felt cornered and couldn't admit he was wrong, so he had done what he always did, he went on the attack. He walked to the door prepared to walk through it, possibly for the last time, with all his worldly possession in one bag. 'Son,' said Baniti. He paused in the doorway, hope in his heart that his father would see through his bravado. That he would allow him to apologise, allow him to stay. 'Don't come back until you can repay your sister and show some remorse for what you have done.'

Baahir's shoulders slumped slightly before he squared them again. 'Don't hold your breath,' was his parting shot as he walked out the door.

Baniti seemed to sag slightly as Baahir left. With all the anger leaving his system, he seemed to reduce in size in front of Amira's eyes. 'Father,' whispered Amira. 'I'm sorry Father.' Baniti looked at Amira and held out his arms. She ran into them and accepted the hug he was offering and let the tears fall.

'I'm sorry princess,' he said as she cried. He looked over to Anipe who also had tears running down her face. 'I have room for two,' he said gently. With a wobbly smile, she also walked into his embrace.

Amira shook the memories off and opened the wicker basket where she had placed the beautiful shimmering material that Khepri had given her.

Blushing, she remembered Khepri's knowing words that day. It would indeed make a beautiful wedding dress. To Amira's dismay, when she opened the box, it was empty. *Nooooo, it can't be true. Not again ...!* They hadn't seen Baahir since that day, and it had been over six months. It couldn't possibly be him; he couldn't have found her hiding place again. *Please God, no.* With pain in her heart, she clutched the empty basket. She didn't think the material, as beautiful as it was, would be of any interest to him. She had only told her mother about the material, and its intended use, so Baahir didn't even know about it.

She stood on shaking legs and the basket dropped from her numb fingers. She walked as if in a daze into the living area to look for her mother. Anipe was at the kitchen table chopping vegetables, humming gently to herself as she worked. At Amira's entrance she looked up, the smile freezing on her face. 'Amira, what is it sweetie?' She quickly got up from the table and led Amira to the dining chair. Amira gratefully sunk onto the seat and Anipe put a cup of water in front of her.

Amira looked up at her mother with stricken eyes. 'It's gone,' she whispered.

'What has honey?' said Anipe, gently rubbing her back.

'The material.' She paused to compose herself. 'The material that Khepri gave me, for my wedding dress. Baahir? How?'

'Oh honey,' said her mother, giving her a hug. 'I'm so sorry. I should have told you, but I wanted it to be a surprise. Wait here, I'll be back.' Giving Amira another hug, Anipe left the room. She returned quickly with a dress draped over her arm. Amira instantly recognised the beautiful shimmering material that Khepri had given her. Her mother opened the dress up in front of her so that she could see it. 'It's not quite finished yet.' Amira looked at the dress that her mother held. It was beautiful.

'How?' she said, not taking her eyes off the beautiful dress in front of her.

'Your Abubakar came to see your father and I a week ago to ask our permission for your hand. You should have seen him. He was magnificent, and completely petrified,' her mother said, smiling. 'It was obvious to us both how much he loves you. He will look after you, give you a good life, and I know how you feel about him too,' Anipe said, smiling as her daughter blushed.

'I remembered the material you were saving, and I wanted to surprise you. I've been working on it secretly with Ramla. Do you like it?' Anipe asked Amira shyly.

'Oh, Mother, it's beautiful.' With shaking hands, Amira gently touched the shimmering fabric. The dress had a gathered strap which would sit on her left shoulder. It would drape diagonally across her chest under her right arm. There was a thin strap that would hold it in place on her right shoulder. Down the wide strap and along the neckline her mother and Ramla had embroidered a gold vine. There was a larger panel of the design that would sit under her breasts creating a high waistline. The dress then fell elegantly to the floor with more embroidery on the hem. It was exquisite work, and she could tell it was made with love. Looking at her mother with tears running down her face, she swallowed the lump in her throat. 'Thank you, Mama, it is truly beautiful.'

Beaming, Anipe started walking towards Amira's bedroom. 'Come, you must try it on.' Amira quickly followed her into her room and her mother laid the dress across her bed. 'I'll be back in a minute,' she said and left. She came back to find that Amira hadn't moved and was still staring at the dress. Laughing, Anipe looked at Amira. 'It won't break. It won't try itself on either.' Amira looked at her mother with shining eyes and that's when she realised her mother was holding something else. In one hand she had a beautiful pair of white satin slippers with the beginning of embroidery on them. Over her other arm she had a shawl made from the same shimmering material with the gold embroidery along the edges. 'We had some of the material left over,' she said, smiling. She placed the shawl on the bed. 'The shoes still need finishing, but you should try them on with your dress.' After placing them on the floor, she walked towards the door. 'I'm just going to fetch Ramla, she will want to see this. Do you need any help?'

Amira absently shook her head. 'I don't think so,' she said and reverently touched the dress.

Anipe quickly went next door and knocked on Ramla's door, praying that she would be home. Thankfully, she opened the door quickly. Seeing Anipe bouncing on her toes, she laughed at her girlish excitement. 'She is trying on the dress. Are you coming?' she said with a big grin on her face.

Ramla nodded her head vigorously and held up one hand. 'Wait one minute,' she said and disappeared from view. When she came back, she had her shawl and a bottle of liquid. 'A toast for the occasion,' she said, winking at Anipe. Giggling like young girls, Ramla closed the door, and they went back to Anipe's.

Chapter 15 – Amira

Amira could barely sleep for tomorrow she was marrying Abubakar. She desperately wanted to fall asleep because the quicker she fell asleep, the quicker she could wake up and it would be tomorrow. She felt like she had been waiting for this day since she had been a little girl and Abubakar moved in next door. She had looked into his eyes and felt a connection to him she had never felt to another human being.

Feeling restless, she got up and paced around the room. They were at Tifi and Saju's house. Saju had offered his garden for the ceremony as that was where Abubakar had proposed to her. She thought it was very thoughtful of them and they had accepted their kind offer. She, her mother, and her father were staying with Tifi and Saju. Abubakar had asked Ramla to conduct the marriage ceremony being a priestess of their village, and he knew the connection that Ramla and Amira had. Ramla had been delighted to officiate.

Abubakar and his family were staying with Tifi and Saju's neighbours to their left and Ramla was staying with their neighbours to the right. Amira was blown away by the kindness of Tifi and Saju and their neighbours. Abubakar had asked Saju to be his best man, who was honoured to accept, and that is when he had come up with the idea of having the ceremony in his garden.

Amira wasn't allowed outside as the garden had been prepared for the ceremony and she wasn't allowed to see. Chairs and tables were to be set up in the shared courtyard and each neighbour was opening their gardens and homes to accommodate the wedding party and guests. Amira was positively buzzing with excitement. She wished she could see Abubakar. He always knew what to say to her to help her relax. He was the only person who could make her laugh when she thought it wasn't possible. In the absence of Abubakar, just the thought of him had the desired effect. She was marrying the man she had loved since she was a little girl. Any fear she may have felt disappeared, and she felt a calmness wash over her. It just felt right …

She lay down again on the bed breathing in and out slowly, and sleep eventually came.

The next morning dawned and the sun shining through the window awoke her. She got up and went to the window. It looked like it was going to be a beautiful day. She heard movement as others in the house woke up and started moving around. There was a gentle knock on her door, and at her answer, the door opened. Her mother popped her head through. 'Good, you are awake. Good morning honey.'

'Morning Mama. I'm getting married today,' Amira said with a breathy giggle. Anipe walked in and gave her a hug.

There was another knock on the door and Anipe went to open the door wider. A tub was carried in followed by jug after jug of hot water. The tub was filled with steaming fragrant water. Amira breathed in the scent of jasmine. She looked at her mother. 'Ramla made it especially,' said Anipe. Amira felt so lucky to be surrounded by so many loving people. Her mother helped her undress, and she sank into the fragrant water. 'Soak for a little while and I will help you wash your hair.'

Amira savoured the bath, feeling her muscles relax. After a little while her mother came in and helped her wash her hair. It was going to be a warm day and her hair wouldn't need much help drying. Her mother helped her out of the tub and wrapped her in a fluffy towel. The tub was emptied using a drain in the recess and taken from the room.

There was another knock on the door and, at her mother's call, Ramla entered. She was dressed in full priestess regalia and looked amazing. 'Good, I came in time,' she said, passing Amira a small parcel. Amira opened the parcel and within found a nightdress of the shimmering material her wedding dress and shawl were made of. 'Khepri was very generous with the materi-al,' Ramla said. Amira held up the fine nightdress adorned with the same gold embroidery. Ramla and her mother had been busy indeed. There was also a bottle inside. She opened the top and inhaled the fragrant smell of jasmine flowers. 'The nightdress is for tonight,' said Ramla. 'That is for now,' she said, pointing to the bottle.

Amira's heart was full of love and kindness for the two amazing women in front of her. 'Thank you. I love you both so much,' she said.

The other ladies both embraced her with tears in their eyes. 'I love you too,' they both said in unison. Laughing tearily, they hugged each other too.

'I'll leave you to it. See you in a little while,' said Ramla, leaving the room.

Anipe combed some of the fragrant oil through Amira's hair, and then, with cloths, tied it into tight curls and left it to dry. She then massaged more of the oil into Amira's hands, arms, shoulders, back, and legs. She left Amira to finish and went from the room to fetch her dress, shawl, and shoes.

When Amira was ready, she came back in and passed Amira filmy underwear also made from the same fabric. There was a knock on the door and Anipe opened the door to Tifi. She carried in a tray of tea and pastries and placed them on a small table. Smiling, she left them together and mother and daughter drank tea, ate pastries, and talked while Amira's hair dried.

Amira sat while Anipe did her makeup for her. It was her first time having her eyes made up with eyeliner. Her mother helped her into her dress and removed the cloths from her hair so that it fell down her back in waves. She placed the necklace Abubakar had made for her around her neck, and it fitted with the dress as if designed for it. There was another tap on the door and Anipe went to answer it. She came back with something wrapped in cloth and placed it in the palm of Amira's hand. 'From Abubakar,' she said.

Amira opened the cloth and there nestled inside was a comb adorned with a carved jasmine flower, a clear complement to the necklace. Smiling, Amira looked at her mother. Anipe took the comb and, sweeping one side of Amira's hair up, fixed it in place with the comb. Amira stood and put her slippers on her feet. Anipe placed the shawl around her shoulder and Amira let it drop to rest at her elbows. 'You are ready. You look beautiful honey.' Her mother's shining eyes matched her shining smile. She slipped out of the room to let everyone know that Amira was ready, and Amira composed herself. She looked at the young woman in the mirror and barely recognised the poised lady smiling back at her.

As the door opened, she made her way towards it. Her father was standing in the corridor swallowing up all the space. 'You look beautiful,' he said and kissed her gently on one cheek. 'Are you ready?' At Amira's nod he handed her a bouquet of jasmine which Amira took. Taking her other hand, he led her to the doorway. Stepping outside, she took his arm and they walked towards the opened gate to the garden, where Abubakar was waiting for them.

As she stepped into the garden on her father's arm, she breathed in the fragrance of the flowers. They had transformed the already beautiful garden, adding pots of jasmine flowers. They had strung up colourful lanterns around the outside wall which they would light later for guests to mill about. As her father led her around the path, she could hear water gently trickling into the pond.

When they walked around the bend in the path towards the straight, there in front of her was Abubakar. Her breath caught at the sight of him. How handsome he looked. Abubakar was standing under an arch which had been erected for their wedding with jasmine flowers entwined around it. Everything was beautiful. Standing beside Abubakar was Saju looking very handsome too.

Tifi stood to one side with her son in her arms, and on the other side was her mother and Abubakar's mother and father. Baniti led her to Abubakar, and he took her hand and placed a kiss on her palm. 'You look beautiful,' he said.

Amira passed her bouquet to Anipe, and they turned to face Ramla who smiled gloriously at them both. At her instruction they faced each other with Amira's hand clasped in Abubakar's. She wrapped a ribbon around their clasped hands and around each of their wrists binding them together. She then called on the gods to bless their union and asked both parents to bless their union. She called upon Abubakar to take Amira as his wife and Amira to take Abubakar as her husband.

She then read a poem entwining them together as friends, lovers, and soul mates and blessed their union with love, happiness, and health. Jasmine petals were thrown up in the air and gently cascaded around them. Abubakar softly kissed Amira on the lips pledging his life to her, and Amira pledged her life to him.

They turned to the applause of their friends and family and were kissed and hugged by proud fathers and teary mothers. They turned and the gate was opened to the courtyard. Abubakar led Amira through to the courtyard, which had also been beautifully transformed, to more applause from their neighbours who had made the journey to join them on their special day. Tables and chairs had been laid out around the courtyard. More lanterns had been strung up, and in the middle of each table was a pot of jasmine flowers, with several candles adorning their surface.

As they were congratulated, hugged, and kissed, food and drink were brought out on trays and soon the tables were bursting. Abubakar's father made a speech welcoming Amira into their family and Amira's father toasted next, followed by Saju as Abubakar's best man and then Abubakar himself.

They were blown away by all the people who had made the journey to be there with them on their special day, and by the kindness of Tifi and Saju and their neighbours who had opened their homes to accommodate them all. There were no words that could cover all their thanks, although they did their best to try and articulate their gratitude.

Everyone milled around, chatted, and drank. People wandered through the courtyard and gardens and there was a relaxed buzz in the air. As night fell the lanterns were lit and music signalled time for dancing. Abubakar led Amira to the middle of the courtyard where space had been left for dancing. He took her into his arms and the crowd cheered. Soon there were bodies swaying along to the music in every available space.

'Happy?' asked Abubakar. Amira looked into his eyes.

'Do you really need to ask?' Smiling, Amira stood on tiptoe and kissed Abubakar shyly. 'I feel so blessed,' she said.

'This is just the beginning,' said Abubakar.

Chapter 16 – Emma

Emma was giving herself a pep talk in the mirror above her washbasin in her dorm room. 'You can do this; you can do this,' repeating the words like a mantra hoping it would help calm her nerves.

She was to present her project today in class for her Egyptology course and she couldn't remember the last time she had been this nervous. Hence the pep-talk in the mirror. She would normally have relied on her mom Chione for that, but she was at work and currently unavailable. Emma had spoken to her the night before but hadn't realised at the time how nervous she was going to feel. *What would mom say*? she thought to herself.

She took a deep breath and closed her eyes trying to calm herself. When she opened her eyes, however, it wasn't her own face in front of her. 'I can do this,' said the reflection, and then startled chocolate brown eyes met green.

'Amira?' Emma said tentatively. 'Ami, is that you?'

Recognition replaced the startled expression on her friend's face. 'Emma is that you?' Both friends drank in the reflection of their much-cherished childhood friend, taking in all the differences that time had brought, taking them from children into the young women they were.

Amira had grown into a beautiful young woman. With soulful brown eyes, long dark hair, and a slight build, she still only came up to Emma's midriff. She still had her stubborn chin, although gentle and kind. Emma remembered the stubborn side of her friend well, which she remarked on, making Amira laugh.

Emma was tall at a young age and now reached nearly six foot as an adult, taking after her father in looks. She had beautiful, teasing green eyes and always had a smile on the edge of her mouth. With long blonde hair and a sun-kissed complexion, they were quite a pair: total opposites and beautiful in their own right.

Emma could see that Amira was wearing what looked like a white filmy dress and had the most unusual and beautiful necklace around her neck. She was currently fiddling with it. Catching Emma looking at it, she smiled and dropped it to fall just between her breasts.

'I got married today,' she said, smiling, her eyes twinkling with joy.

'To Abu?' Emma stated. Laughing at her friend's childhood nickname for her beloved husband, Amira nodded her head. Emma could feel the waves of happiness radiating from her friend and was overjoyed. She remembered their many conversations about Abu as children and the childhood crush her friend had had on the boy next door. 'Congratulations Ami, I am so happy for you. I know how much you love him.'

Amira smiled radiantly. 'Thank you, Em.' Amira glanced behind her, and when she looked back at Emma, she looked nervous and started to fiddle with her necklace again.

'Ami, is everything ok? You don't regret getting married, do you?'

'No,' Amira stated firmly, unsure what to say, how to explain her nervousness. *This is Emma*, she told herself. They had shared many secrets over the years, and she trusted her friend. 'Tonight is my wedding night,' she blurted out, blushing with embarrassment.

Emma smiled encouragingly. 'You love Abubakar,' she said. Amira smiled and nodded her head. Emma thought for a moment. She wanted to help and reassure her friend. Then she remembered what her mom had once said to her. 'Mom said to me the instincts come from your heart, the rest will follow as love will lead the way.' Her friend thought about this and seemed to relax slightly. 'Oh, and she said enjoy, then gave me a cheeky smile and a wink.' They looked at each other and laughed again.

'I am so grateful for your mom Emma. She has taught me so much and she doesn't even know it. Did the advice help you?'

Emma thought on this for a moment and blushed herself. 'I haven't found the one yet.'

Amira looked at Emma intently, and then with a secret smile that Emma remembered well, she said, 'You have, it's just timing. By the way,' she said before Emma could ask for more information, 'you will knock their socks off with your presentation my friend so there is no need to worry.' Emma laughed at her friend's choice of words. Amira started to fade and sadly they both knew their time together was about to run out.

'Good luck Ami.'

'Good luck Emma.'

'See you soon I hope,' they both said and blew each other a kiss.

Chapter 17 – Amira

'Amira.' Amira turned around to find Abubakar had come into the room. Blushing, she looked over her shoulder at the mirror.

'I was just talking to …' she was unsure how to continue.

'Your friend Emma? Your childhood friend,' he said gently. She looked up at him in surprise, fiddling with her necklace, a habit she seemed to have acquired ever since he had given it to her when he proposed. When she felt nervous, it made her feel safe, as if his love and protection were radiating from the very stone. He smiled at her. A gentle, loving smile. 'You forget that I have known you for a long time. I pay attention.

Maybe you could tell me about her sometime,' said Abubakar.

'Really?' asked Amira. She looked like such a lost child when she said it, he couldn't help but take her in his arms.

He drew back and picked up the amulet hanging from the chain around her neck. 'I meant what I said when I gave you this. I love you, all of you. That includes your gift. I will protect you with my name, my reputation, heart, body, and soul.'

Amira looked at the man she loved with tears and love shining from her eyes. She remembered the boy she had fallen in love with who had protected her from spiders and shadows. She loved him with all her heart and knew how much he loved her in return.

With Amira looking at him like that, Abubakar couldn't help himself; he kissed her gently on the lips. He had loved her for so long, since he had first seen her as a shy little girl. All he wanted to do was protect her and love her.

He waited, holding his breath, seeing what she would do. Would she pull away uncertain of his kiss? She looked up at him and surprised him by standing up on tiptoe to kiss him boldly on the mouth. He was so proud of how she was trying to overcome her shyness and delighted at her boldness. Seeing his surprise and delight, she did it again. This time, as she went to step away, he gathered her close to him. Moulding her body to his, he deepened the kiss.

He gently touched her bottom lip with his tongue to see how she would react. Amira sighed into his mouth, so he gently touched the end of her tongue with his. She made a surprised noise in the back of her throat and pressed her body closer to his. He stood back, chuckling slightly, and drank in the beautiful face cupped between his hands.

She looked at him and he could see that she was coming to some kind of decision. She placed her hands on his chest and stood on tiptoe until her lips were just a breath away from his. 'Show me how much you love me,' she whispered.

With his heart thudding in his chest, he lifted her hands up to place a kiss on the centre of each palm, making her shiver. Tingles and warmth shot up Amira's arms spreading through her body. As Abubakar led her to the bed, she decided to heed Emma's mom's advice and let love lead the way.

Abubakar wanted this to be special for Amira. This being her first time, he wanted to be able to go slow and allow Amira to get used to his touch; he wanted to show her the stars. Amira wouldn't allow him to be in control, wouldn't let him think or go slow as he had intended. After the next drugging kiss, he was unable to think at all. So, he undressed her, worshipping her with his eyes, his lips, and his hands, and when she reached the stars, he was right there alongside her.

Chapter 18 – Emma and Kyle

Emma and Kyle ran back into the tent just in time. A sandstorm had come up unexpectedly and they hoped that the artefacts they had partly uncovered would be safe. There was nothing to do but wait out the storm and assess the damage after.

Kyle found himself face to face with Emma, looking into her dancing eyes. His own heart was pounding from the adrenaline of their find and the mad dash into the tent.

This was their first dig together, although they had been communicating by internet and phone for about six months. Being this close to Emma, he could see the gold flecks in the depths of her eyes. She was breathing heavily from their mad dash, and he could feel her breath on his face with them being in such close quarters.

Kyle could feel the rush of adrenaline heat his blood, and his heart was beating faster, not just due to his run but also due to Emma's closeness. They had become good friends through their communication, and he enjoyed their easy friendship. They both sensed the attraction between them, but this was the first time that they had felt it physically in each other's presence.

He saw Emma's pupils widen and knew in that moment that she felt the attraction too. Like two magnets were pulling them together, they leaned towards each other. Just as their lips were about to connect in what would be their first kiss, Bradley shouted, 'Watch out!' as he barrelled through the tent flap coughing and spluttering, bringing what felt like a wall of sand with him.

'Close that flap you idiot,' shouted someone from behind them.

'Not interrupting anything I hope?' said Bradley, winking at Emma and Kyle. They immediately stepped back from each other, Emma going red in the face and Kyle wanting to happily strangle Bradley for his thoughtlessness.

It became apparent that they had not been alone. Everything else around them had seemed to melt away in that moment and all that was left was Emma and Kyle's desire to kiss each other. They looked at each other sheepishly and both smiled. The tension melted away and they sat down to wait out the storm, sinking into easy conversation, both feeling desire still singing in their blood.

Kyle contemplated how he could arrange to finish that kiss. They were staying on the site for the next couple of nights, but the men would be in one tent and the women in the other. There wouldn't be much chance for privacy.

They received the ok to resume their dig and went back out to assess the damage the storm had caused to their site. They would normally have covered their areas over before leaving them, but with the storm coming in unexpectedly, they hadn't had time. Looking around them, they could see broken pottery that they had dug up earlier and placed ready to be cleaned and boxed.

Other parts of the site had been covered with sand and they would have to start again. 'This will set us back a few hours,' said Tom their camp leader. 'Any explanation for how the storm got past you?' said Tom, looking directly at Bradley. Bradley just shrugged. 'I think we need to talk,' said Tom, and they watched Bradley follow him reluctantly into one of the tents.

Emma picked up a piece of the pottery. 'Do you think you can fix it?' said Kyle.

'I won't know until it is cleaned,' said Emma. Emma had a knack for restoration and wanted this to be part of her career. Kyle knew that her ability and love for this field came from her mom Chione who also did art restoration. Emma used to watch her and sometimes help when she went into work with her at the Rosicrucian Egyptian Museum.

The rest of the days at the dig seemed to fly past, and before they knew it, they were at the airport. They said goodbye to everyone else and there was only the two of them left. This was the first time they had been alone since that near kiss. As much as he had tried, Kyle hadn't had a chance to get Emma alone to discuss it, or to finish what they had started.

He racked his brain for what to say and shuffled his feet slightly. This was the first time that he had felt awkward in her presence. Their flights were called for boarding over the tannoy. Their time had run out and Kyle felt his heart sink. Then, much to his delight, Emma stood up on tiptoe and kissed him.

He felt the kiss right down to his toes. Emma swayed back and he grasped her upper arms gently and deepened the kiss. Emma sighed into his mouth. They drew back and gave each other a wobbly smile.

'Have a safe journey,' they said at the same time.

'You too,' they both said at the same time again. They both laughed.

'Great minds,' Kyle said. 'Speak soon. Goodbye Em,' he said, cupping her cheek gently in his hand.

'Goodbye Kyle,' said Emma, and turning, they made their way to their respective gates on wobbly legs with big grins on their faces.

Chapter 19 – Kyle

The first year and a half at university seemed to fly. It was coming to half term and Kyle had an idea, but he wanted to run it by Emma first.

At eight o'clock that night, he called Emma on *Google Duo*. It would be one o'clock in the afternoon for her so she would be home.

Her smiling face came on the screen and his heart leapt as it always did. 'Hi,' she said.

'Hi,' he replied. 'I have an idea. What are you doing for half-term?' he said.

'I'll probably go home to Los Angeles to see mom and dad and hang with some friends and with mom at the museum. What about you?'

'How would you feel if I came to see you?' Kyle's heart was pounding in his chest. What if she didn't want him to visit. This hadn't occurred to him before asking the question. *Maybe this was a bad idea*, he thought. He waited with a dry mouth, but when a delighted look came over her face, he realised he needn't have worried.

Her words came out all jumbled with her excitement. 'How? Can you afford that? Where will you stay?'

He stopped her in her tracks laughing. 'I've been thinking about it for a while. I have money saved from my catering job. I've also pitched it to the university as a part study visit that would help with my course as your mom works at a museum, with the best Egyptian exhibit in America, might I add. I couldn't go on the last dig with the other students, so they have the money set aside from that. They agreed to release it for me if I brought credible study material back with me. I spoke to my parents, and they are happy for me to go because they know how much it would mean to me to see you in person.' He paused for breath. 'I would just need to figure out somewhere to stay. What do you think?'

Emma's smile grew wide 'I think that would be amazing. Wait a moment.' She left the screen, and he heard her muffled voice talking on the phone. She sat back down beaming. 'I've just spoken to mom and dad. Do you remember Professor Wakefield, mom's friend at the museum?

Kyle thought for a moment and then, nodding his head, he said, 'The linguist expert?'

'Yes,' Emma said. 'Well, he only lives a few streets away and mom said he has a spare room. She is talking to him now. He is a really cool guy; you will definitely get on with him.'

He heard Emma's phone ring and, after speaking to her mom, she put her on speaker phone. 'Hi Kyle,' she said.

'Hi Chione, how are you?' He had long been told to call both Emma's parents by their first names and he felt comfortable doing so.

'Good,' she said, 'good. I've just spoken to Mark, and he said he would be happy to put you up. You can have your meals with us if you would like. We would be happy to have you.'

Kyle's heart soared at their kindness. Without having to find money for a room and food, he knew that he could make the visit happen. 'Thank you so much, I would like that very much Chione. Thank you for your hospitality and thank Professor Wakefield for me too.'

'You are very welcome,' said Chione. 'We are very much looking forward to seeing you in person. I will leave you both to it. Take care Kyle. We will see you soon.'

Smiling, with tears in her eyes, Emma said, 'This is really happening.' Feeling a little choked himself, he nodded his head. They talked particulars for a little while longer and, blowing her a kiss, he said goodbye.

Kyle visited his parents that weekend and filled them in on his plans, telling them about the kind offer of Emma's parents and friend. He saw his mum and dad share a look and his dad left the room. He came back after just a few moments and handed him an envelope. Holding his wife's hand, he smiled at his son. With curiosity, Kyle opened the envelope.

Inside he found a return plane ticket to LA. He looked up at his proud and beaming parents.

'Chione called us on Thursday to say how delighted she was to be meeting you in person. We told her we wanted to surprise you with the ticket, so we ironed out travel details there and then. Matthew will pick you up from the airport and drop you back when you are ready to come home,' his dad said.

Kyle didn't know what to say. With four sons to look after, he knew his parents didn't have a lot of spare money and he was overwhelmed that they had done this for him. 'Thank you,' he said, shaking his dad's hand and giving him a hug. 'Thank you,' he said, kissing his mum on the cheek and giving her a hug also.

Dabbing the tears running down her face with his shirt sleeve, his mum said, 'We are so proud of you and how hard you have been working. We wanted to do this for you.'

On his trip with Emma, they visited the museum where Emma's mom and her mom's friend Mark worked. Emma gave him the grand tour leaving her favourite exhibition until last. They had spent what felt like hours looking at the Egyptian artefacts when she took his hand and led him to a case in the centre of the room which was lit from within. 'I remember visiting this every holiday when I was a child. Every time I come back here; I feel drawn to it. It is from a private collector who lends it to the museum for three months every year, along with other artefacts from his collection, in exchange for cleaning and restoration. I am lucky that it always coincided with my holidays.'

Kyle stood in front of the glass case transfixed. 'You never sent me a leaflet of this exhibit?'

'We never advertised it as a separate exhibit. I'm not sure why,' Emma said bemused. Kyle couldn't believe it, for there in front of him on display, with just a piece of glass separating them, was the amulet. The one he had held that day at school when he was a child. The same amulet that had transported him back to Egypt. He remembered that day like it was yesterday. He remembered the beautiful owner, he remembered the sand beneath his feet, the heat on his face and body, and he remembered the extraordinary view of a pyramid right in front of his startled eyes. He remembered turning around at a noise and seeing the most beautiful women he had ever seen. He remembered the sorrow in her eyes, the kindness, her eyes beseeching him for help. He remembered that moment so well that it had set his life on its current course.

Emma put a hand on his arm. 'Are you ok? You have gone very pale.' Kyle debated whether to tell her of his experience. He trusted Emma and, somehow, he didn't know why, inside he knew she would understand. She wouldn't make fun of him. She wouldn't think he was mad.

'Can I tell you something? Something that I have never told anyone else.' Emma looked at Kyle's face and then back at the amulet he had been looking at so intently. He was positively vibrating with emotion.

She nodded her head. 'Why don't we take a walk.' She took his hand and guided him out through the back of the museum only used by staff members. In the warm sunlight she felt his tension ebb slightly. She smiled encouragingly at him, and he began his story. He told her about Professor O'Hare's visit to the school and his experience after taking hold of the amulet. He told her about his need to find out about the owner of the necklace and the feeling he had that, even at a young age, she was asking for his help. He told her about the mysterious benefactor who had paid for his scholarship which allowed him to go to university to study archaeology.

Emma listened intently feeling that they had been led to each other for a reason. Feeling honoured that he had trusted her with something he had never told anyone else for fear of being ridiculed, she felt it was right to do the same.

So, she told him of her imaginary friend as a child called Amira. The girl with the strange clothes who talked differently to her. She told him of the dreams that she had when she saw through Amira's eyes into her life. He listened intently and, when she paused, he asked, 'Do you think it is the same person?'

Emma nodded. 'I haven't thought about her for years, but when I started university, the dreams and visions started again. I saw her last year in my bathroom mirror. She must be about sixteen maybe; she looked just as you described. I remember her wearing a necklace; it looked familiar at the time, but I didn't connect it until now.'

'Let's sit down.' Kyle led Emma over to a bench where they both sat in silence, both digesting what they had shared.

'Why do you think this is happening? Why us? What for?' whispered Emma.

'I don't know,' said Kyle. 'I guess only time will tell.'

After a moment he had a thought. 'Do you think I could hold the necklace?

'It's due to be cleaned tomorrow. It will be your only chance for at least six months. It is always cleaned before we send it back to the owner.'

The timing hadn't escaped them – the fact he had chosen to visit that week when the exhibit was still there. 'I will ask mom. Do you think it will happen again?'

'I don't know. It might not happen again, but it feels important to try,' said Kyle.

Emma spoke to her mom that night. Chione was aware of her daughter's gifts, more so than Emma herself. When Emma said it was important, Chione said she would make the arrangements. Kyle and Emma went to the museum the next day and she led him through to the back area of the museum that visitors didn't see. Staff were bustling around receiving and packing up exhibits, cataloguing and cleaning. It was fascinating and Kyle saw a little bit of what his future world would hold.

They found Chione in a room on her own. There in the centre was a velvet case, and sitting nestled inside was the amulet. It seemed to twinkle in the overhead lighting, drawing him forward. There were two pairs of white material gloves next to the case on the table with various cleaning apparatus spread out around it in reach ready to be used.

'If anyone asks, I've been called away to sort an emergency situation and I asked you to stay as I didn't want to leave the necklace unattended,' said Chione. 'I have given you permission to handle it if anyone asks.'

'Thank you, Mom,' Emma said and, squeezing her hand, Chione left.

Kyle cautiously approached the bench with Emma and sat down. They put their gloves on, and Emma took the necklace out of the case. 'People are used to seeing me here so we shouldn't have a problem. I can see that mom was dying to stay and see,' Emma said smiling.

'What if it doesn't work?' Kyle said with concern in his voice. He also felt foolish. *What if nothing happened? What if it had been a fluke? What if he had imagined it all?*

Emma, sensing his turmoil, squeezed his hand and he felt himself relax. 'Ready?' she asked. Kyle took a deep breath and, nodding, he held out his hands feeling more composed.

Kyle blinked a few times until Emma came back into focus. 'Did it work?' she asked. Kyle nodded his head slowly, feeling too dizzy to speak. 'You look a bit green,' Emma said, concerned. 'Wait here a moment,' she said, leaving the room. She came back with Chione who looked at him with worry. 'Come with me,' Emma said, and taking his hand gently, she led him to the nearest rest room. She left him to splash water on his face and came back with a glass of water and a couple of ginger biscuits. He took them gratefully, and after sipping the water and eating the biscuits, he felt a little better.

'Did anything happen on your end?' he asked.

'Not much,' said Emma. 'You went very still like you were in a trance. I think I almost expected you to disappear in a puff of smoke,' she said sheepishly.

'Let's get a coffee and something to eat and I will fill you in.' They left the museum and Emma took him to a coffee shop where they could talk. They sat in a quiet corner where they wouldn't be overheard, and Kyle told her everything he could remember of what happened.

Chapter 20 – Amira

There was a strange man in her garden. He was wearing unusual clothes that she could only remember ever seeing once before.

She stepped outside cautiously and he turned. He looked just as confused as he had done before, for she knew she would recognise him anywhere. The same blue eyes, the same brown hair which flopped over his forehead, and then he smiled, and she remembered that smile most of all.

'It's you,' they both said in unison, and both laughed nervously.

Kyle looked at Amira in shock. 'You speak English! How?' And then it dawned on him. 'Emma,' he whispered.

Her face lit up. 'You know Emma? Of course,' she said, smiling. 'That makes sense, you are the one she had been waiting for.

I have seen so much through her eyes. She has taught me so much and given me more than she will ever know. I call it my secret weapon from my friend with the biggest heart. My secret weapon from my heart. My name is Amira. What is yours? I think we are going to be friends too.'

'Kyle,' he said, and he gave her that smile again. 'I have thought about you a lot since I met you that time as a boy. I've wondered who you were, what happened to you, and how I came to be here in the first place. That first time I met you I felt as though you were asking me for help. Is that silly? It's because of you that I am studying to become an archaeologist.'

At her confused look, he explained what that meant. Amira listened and then nodded and smiled. 'You seek to find out about the past. You wish to become a Truth Seeker.

Kyle thought for a moment and then nodded his head. 'A Truth Seeker. I like that.' She looked at his hand and noticed that he once again had her necklace in his hand.

'I didn't realise that I lost it again. Yet here you are returning it. It seems I am destined to keep losing it,' she said.

Kyle looked at the amulet nestled in the palm of his hand. 'It's beautiful,' he said.

Amira smiled. 'It was an engagement gift from Abubakar, my husband. It was his pledge to me that he will love me, all of me, everything about me, and that he will be my protector. The flower is jasmine. It is my favourite flower, and he says that whenever he smells jasmine, he thinks of me. The symbol is the Eye of Horus, and the gemstone is malachite. He recognises my gift as a seer and promises to protect me. He made it for me; it is one of a kind.'

Kyle felt drawn to hand the amulet over, as if it were ready to go home to its rightful owner. With reluctance, he held out his hand and Amira took the necklace from him. 'My Truth Seeker,' she said. 'Say hello to Emma, My Heart.'

Chapter 21 – Amira

Amira was heading home from the market where she had bought supplies to cook Abubakar his favourite meal. They had been married for a couple of months and she was settling into her role as wife nicely. She was so happy and content and was humming a happy tune to herself as she made her way home.

As she approached the house, she saw a familiar figure standing at the door. She shielded her eyes to see him better and her step faltered as she recognised who it was. Her heart started to beat faster, and she felt a little sick, for standing on her doorstep was her brother Baahir.

She hadn't seen Baahir since the day their father had sent him from the house. Just seeing him there brought back all of the hurtful words he had said to her that day. She wished Abubakar was here. Why couldn't he have waited until later when they were together? But no, here he was. Knowing her brother, he had probably planned it this way so that he had the upper hand.

She was so tempted to turn around and walk away and pretend that she hadn't seen him. As if sensing her hesitation, Baahir stepped forward, his hands splayed wide. 'Hello Amira. I haven't come to cause trouble, I promise.' Amira looked at him without words, assessing the changes that time had made on his person. He looked thinner than she remembered. His boyish good looks had gone and in their place were the hard lines of a cynical man.

She could see that he was assessing her too. 'I hear congratulations are in order. You look happy,' said Baahir.

'Thank you,' said Amira. 'Why are you here Baahir? Why now?'

Baahir turned around and picked a box up from her step. 'Mother told me about you and Abubakar getting married. I wanted to congratulate you and bring you a gift.' He held it out to Amira, but she didn't take it, so he awkwardly placed it back on the step. At Amira's quizzical gaze, he explained. 'Mother wrote to me about Father being ill. I guess she thought I might want to make peace with him.'

'That was three months ago,' said Amira. 'We were very worried about him, but Father is strong and thankfully he pulled through. Mother could have done with your support then.' She could see Baahir bristling under her words. There was no reprimand in her voice, but her words were true, and she wasn't going to take them back. 'Why now Baahir?' It seemed he had no answer to give her, and Amira felt a wave of foreboding.

Ignoring her question, Baahir started to walk around her garden looking at her plants and herbs. 'I finally made enough money to pay you back,' he said. 'It's in there.' He pointed to the box on the step. Surprised, Amira looked at him, but there was more, she could sense it. That wasn't his reason for coming back. 'I'm doing well at last. I have a good business venture I wanted to talk to Father about and maybe Abubakar and his father might be interested too. They could make a good profit on it.'

So, he wanted some investors. 'I'm sure you have new friends that could invest in your venture. Have you not made contacts in your new life?' It was true that Baahir had finally made something of himself. In fact, it had been his plan to come back and gloat about how well he was doing.

When he had knocked on what he thought was still his parents' house and was redirected to a much grander dwelling, he knew what he had accomplished was nothing compared to what he had walked away from. He knew that his father was a good businessman, but he never expected this. His father together with Khnurn had built their business up and had a very good reputation. All this had fallen into Abubakar's lap. It could have been his, but he had been denied it.

It was standing on his father and mother's doorstep that put the idea into his head. He deserved his due; he was part of this family too, and if they didn't include him in their business, then they could at least help him in his. So instead of gloating, he decided to make amends, say he was sorry and be welcomed back into his family.

His acquaintances had been almost salivating over the ships and produce that had been taking Egypt by storm and he hadn't even realised at the time that it was his family's business about which they were talking. Now he knew he could use the family name to his advantage. He deserved to be as successful as them after all.

'I missed my family,' said Baahir. 'It was time to come home. I wanted to say sorry for what I did to you and what I said that day. I hurt you and I didn't mean it. I felt trapped and I lashed out at you. Please accept my apology.'

Amira had a big heart and wanted to believe that Baahir was sincere, but she wasn't that trusting little girl anymore that looked up to her brother and followed him around. She had been on the end of his spite as an adult now. It made her look back over their childhood and reassess all the experiences where they had submitted to his will. She didn't think she could trust him ever again.

Amira smiled. 'Thank you for your apology,' she said.

Baahir could see that it wouldn't be as easy as he thought. *That's ok*, he thought, *I have time*. 'Mother wanted me to invite you and Abubakar for dinner tomorrow. Maybe I will see you there.' *That's enough for now*, Baahir thought. *I must come up with a plan to win her over.*

Amira watched Baahir swagger away. *What is he up to?* she thought. Stepping around the box on the step, she carried her purchases into the kitchen not ready to look in it yet.

She started to prepare dinner, no longer humming to herself. She felt rattled by Baahir's visit and couldn't wait for Abubakar to come home.

Abubakar couldn't wait to get home. It had been a long day, and he was looking forward to going home to his wife. His wife. He would never get over the feeling of how proud he felt at the thought of Amira being his wife. His men had started to rib him about how many times he slipped the word wife into conversation. They could see how happy he was and didn't rib him too hard as they said they would let him off, being a newlywed.

His step quickened as he got closer to home. He had some gemstones and herb cuttings as a gift for Amira. Humming to himself, he turned the last corner towards home.

As he approached the house, he could see a box on the front step. He picked it up and opened the front door ready to greet his wife with a kiss. He could smell dinner in the air and his stomach grumbled at the delicious smells.

Abubakar put the parcel on the table and called Amira's name. He frowned when there was no answer and went to check the bedroom. She wasn't in there either. *She is probably in her garden,* he thought.

He stepped outside and, to his delight, there she was digging in the soil. At the sound of footsteps behind her, Amira quickly turned around, and at the sight of him, she jumped up, wiped the soil off her hands onto her apron, and ran towards him. He opened his arms in time and stopped them both from toppling over at the force of her body hitting his.

'I'm so glad you are home,' she said, gripping him in a fierce hug.

'Amira, what's wrong?' said Abubakar, sensing straight away that something was amiss. Amira lifted her troubled face to Abubakar, and he kissed her gently on the mouth. 'Let's go inside,' he said. Gently, he led her into the house, and she sat at the table. 'Do you want any water?' he asked. At Amira's nod, he poured her a glass and, passing it to her, sat opposite her at the table.

She took a sip and put the cup down on the table. Abubakar held her hand in his and gave it a gentle squeeze. 'What is it, Amira? You can tell me,' he said. Amira looked at him as one single tear escaped from her brimming eyes and slipped down her face unnoticed by her. Abubakar reached out and wiped the tear away. 'Amira, honey, what's wrong?'

Amira took a deep breath. 'Baahir … he … he … is back,' she hiccupped. 'He turned up today out of the blue.' She proceeded to fill Abubakar in on his visit. Abubakar glanced at the box that he had taken from the step and put on the table. Amira was looking at it like a snake had slithered in and set up home. Sensing she didn't want to open the box herself, Abubakar squeezed her hand again and reached for it.

He opened the lid cautiously and peered inside. It did indeed contain money, a mixture of gold coins and doubloons. 'I don't want it,' said Amira. 'It comes with a price I am sure, and not one I wish to pay.' Abubakar lifted Amira up and held her on his lap. She sunk into his embrace, feeling safe once more. 'I won't let him hurt you again,' said Abubakar. He placed a kiss on the top of her head. 'We will go to dinner tomorrow night and see what he is up to. I also have contacts I can reach out to. I don't want you to worry anymore.'

Abubakar held Amira for a while longer enjoying the feel of her in his arms. She relaxed in his embrace, and he felt content. Trying to regain some of his earlier mood, he said, 'What is that delicious smell?'

Amira looked up at him smiling, 'Your favourite. Why don't you wash up while I lay the table?' She leaned up for a kiss and then got up off his lap. He promptly dragged her back down for another kiss.

'Will it keep?' he said, as he started to nibble her neck.

Giggling, Amira nodded her head. 'Just let me place the covers.' She leapt up and did that. As she finished, Abubakar came up behind her and looped his arms around her middle, placing sweet kisses down her neck. She sank back into his arms with a sigh, all thoughts of Baahir's visit and dinner forgotten for now.

Abubakar lifted her up into his arms and carried her through to their bedroom. He proceeded to kiss and undress her until she had no thoughts but him.

Chapter 22 – Baahir

Baahir was enjoying his newfound prestige. He bandied about his father's and Khnurn's names without shame. Doors that had been closed to him before now opened, and he had opportunities and contacts he had never had before. This was his right, he decided. He should have been part of this from the start; it was a family business, and he was family. Why should only Abubakar thrive from their father's business ventures?

He had thought to go to his parents and gloat about how well he was doing, but an opportunity presented itself. His father was poorly so it would be completely plausible for Baahir to want to make amends with him and to return home. Standing on the doorstep of their new home, his plans changed. Maybe if he went to his parents contrite and apologise to Amira, his father would capitulate and take him into the business. Upon his return he found that his father was on the mend. His parents told him that Amira and Abubakar had married. This gave him the perfect reason to see Amira. He would congratulate her on her marriage to Abubakar and repay the money he had taken all those years ago.

He could see at once that it wasn't going to be as easy as he thought. Amira had grown up since their last meeting. She was now married to Abubakar and had helped many people with her healing. He could see this in her demeanour; she wouldn't easily believe what he told her. He could see the distrust on her face, although she tried to mask it.

When she first saw him, he thought that she would bolt. Maybe she needed some time to get over the shock of seeing him. Baahir had tried to reassure her that he wasn't there to cause trouble. He tried to give her the gift he had brought with him, but she didn't move. It was as if she was rooted to the spot.

Seeing she wasn't ready to forgive him, he decided to make a swift exit and move forward with the rest of his plan. He would need to persuade his parents how sorry he was and how he wanted to work hard for the family business. *He should have brought a wife with him*, he thought. That probably would have swayed them more. Made them realise he was ready to settle down in one spot and make something of himself. He had many debts against his name. He needed this; he deserved this. He was part of this family too and they had turned their backs on him, not the other way around.

He could feel his anger simmering under the surface. He squashed it down. It wouldn't serve him to show this to his parents. He didn't have long to speak to them as Abubakar and Amira had been invited to dinner later.

It had all been working fine until Abubakar and Khnurn had stuck their noses in, he thought, anger simmering in his gut. The day after talking to his parents and the dinner with Abubakar and Amira, Abubakar and Khnurn had a meeting with his father. He wasn't invited to attend, and it was held at Khnurn's home so he couldn't even eavesdrop.

He knew as soon as his father came home and the look on his face that he wasn't going to be invited to join the business. Both Khnurn and Abubakar had many business contacts; they knew of his debts and his reputation, and they informed his father. Baniti already knew of course but wanted to believe that his son had changed and was genuine in his apology and the reason for his return. He was getting older and wanted to make peace with his son.

It had taken Baahir three months to come and see him even though he knew how poorly he was. Oh, he had come up with a plausible excuse of travelling and how he hadn't received the missive that Anipe had sent. However, as soon as Baniti had looked into his son's eyes, he knew he was lying. He did not like or trust the man standing in front of him. He had hard, unkind eyes and it saddened Baniti that his son had turned out this way. His son had let hate and discontent into his heart. He was self-ish and he wouldn't let him destroy his family with his schemes.

Straightening his shoulders, because, gods help him, he felt a little afraid of this man in front of him, he named a figure to his son and saw the gleam of greed in his eye. 'You're paying me to go away?' said Baahir. He tried for accusation and shock but didn't entirely pull it off. His mind was already buzzing with the possibilities of what he could do with such a sum.

'That is my final offer,' said Baniti. 'That is your share of the business. I have written out a letter that you will sign agreeing to me buying you out of the business.' The greed in Baahir grew and he very much wanted to ask for more. The truth was he didn't want to work for the business. This gave him an out with a very tidy fee indeed. He eagerly signed the letter.

'Come back tomorrow for the money,' said Baniti. 'I hope you find happiness son, but I fear that you will never have enough and that you don't have a place in your heart for love and contentment. Make some excuse to your mother of why you need to leave.' Baniti took one last look at the man standing in front of him and, with sadness in his heart, he turned his back on him and walked out of the door. He couldn't bear to look at him one moment longer.

Baahir stood there after his father had left. A small part of him, the little boy that he was, that looked up to his father, wanted to call him back. He wanted to tell him that he was truly sorry and wanted to be a better man, wanted his father to be proud of him. But his greed was stronger, so he squashed that part of himself down and walked out of the door. He would speak to his mother before he left tomorrow.

So, with the help of the money given to him by his father, together with the use of his father's name, which he hadn't been given permission to use, he was doing very well for himself thank you very much. Nobody needed to know that he wasn't actually working for his father. His father's name had a lot of sway, and he had a right to use it.

Chapter 23 – Amira

Amira loved working on her land, especially when she had had a restless night due to disturbing dreams. She loved the feel of the soil under her hands, and it helped her to stay grounded. She felt the last vestiges of the dream melting away as she cleared the weeds from around the plants.

She loved watching her plants grow and harvesting her crop when it was ready. Her garden was a far cry from the small piece of land her father had bestowed on her as a child. She now had plots dedicated to fruit and veg, potatoes, grains, and, of course, her herbs. She had been gifted with cuttings over the years from her growing number of clients and some of them were rare indeed.

Ramla had taught her how to take cuttings and encourage new growth. Abubakar had built her a structure where she could work. There was an area where she could hang and dry her herbs, shelves for containers of dried herbs, and a counter where she could cut and crush her herbs to mix into potions. She also had shelves full of bottles and pots, some empty, ready to use, and others already filled with potions and balms. She loved her little workshop and would lose track of time working away in it.

Amira lent back on her heels to rub her back and mop her brow in the afternoon sun. She was heavily pregnant with their first child and couldn't spend much time in her garden the closer the birth got. Abubakar was keeping an annoying, but loving, close eye on her. As if he sensed her thoughts, he appeared at her side, and with his help, she got awkwardly to her feet. 'Don't say it,' she said.

He just looked at her innocently. 'Say what?' And giving her a cheeky grin, he passed her a cup of water. 'Dinner smells delicious; let's go eat,' he said. Leaning on his arm gratefully, she walked back into the shade of the house. He had dished them both up a bowl of steaming stew with some crusty bread and she realised how hungry she was. Sitting down, she tucked in with enthusiasm. Laughing gently, Abubakar gave her a second helping and then sat down himself.

'I received a missive from Ramla today. She is on her way to help you with the birthing. Judging from her letter, she is as excited as us to meet her godchild.'

Amira was relieved. 'Good, I don't think it will be long now. Mother is coming too but I will be glad to have Ramla here. The garden looks good. I didn't have to do much. You have been looking after it for me, although I don't know where you found the time.'

Abubakar smiled at her. 'I sneak out when you are asleep,' he said. The closer Amira got to her birthing, the more tired she became. Abubakar knew how important the gardens were. Not only did they provide food but also an income and, of course, Amira's potions and salves, which she used in her healing.

Chapter 24 – Amira

Two years went past with love and happiness, and Amira once more sat in her garden enjoying a moment of quiet before she prepared for Abubakar getting home. Bay was playing happily by her feet tipping soil from one pot into another and making as much mess as possible. Smiling at him, she rubbed her swollen belly. She had so much to be thankful for and tried to appreciate every day.

A worried frown creased the skin between her brows and anxiety took the shine off her smile. She had had the dream again last night. She had woken up with a scream on her lips and no Abubakar to comfort her. Baahir flitted in and out of their lives as he wished, and whenever he was around, he triggered the nightmare once more.

After every nightmare, Abubakar would comfort her, and they would go over every detail looking for clues. She couldn't see herself in the nightmare so had no idea how old she was. She tried to think of any sounds or any differences in their bedroom which might alert them to a time when the event was to take place. Abubakar tried to convince them both that it was just a dream, but they both knew better. They became more frustrated until Abubakar would drop the subject, worried that it would distress her and the baby.

Abubakar kept a closer eye on her to make sure she rested and ate properly. She treasured these moments of solitude, and the garden was the one place she felt totally relaxed. It annoyed her that the nightmare and Baahir had crept into her place of solitude, and she needed to take control in some way.

'Bay, sweetie, Mama just needs to get some parchment from the house and then we will be right back out. OK sweetie?' Bay nodded his head and held up his pudgy arms for her to pick him up. Smiling indulgently at her son, Amira shook her head. 'Mama can't pick you up at the moment sweetie. Can you walk for Mama?' With a determined look on his little face, he held up one hand for Amira. Amira pulled gently and he stood up on wobbly legs, smiling triumphantly at his mother. 'Well done sweetie,' said Amira, and they walked slowly back to the house.

Bay sat on the step where Amira could see him, and she quickly gathered parchment, ink, and quill, and taking Bay's hand, they walked back to the garden. Bay went back to playing with his pots and Amira sat down and contemplated what she wanted to write.

How far should she go back? she thought. Putting ink to parchment, Amira started to write. She wrote about her parents and Baahir and their life growing up. She wrote about Emma and their playtimes together, as well as seeing her on her wedding night. She wrote about her Truth Seeker and anything she could remember about his visits. Lastly, she wrote about the nightmares.

When she had finished, Amira felt more relaxed and in control of an uncontrollable situation. She looked up at the placement of the sun in the sky. 'Daddy will be home soon Bay sweetie. Let's go prepare dinner.'

Bay looked up at her from the ground and clapped his hands. 'Dad, Dad, Dad, home,' he gurgled happily.

'I agree,' said Amira. She gathered the writing supplies, and taking Bay's hand, they went into the house. Amira would show Abubakar what she had written later that night and happily started to prepare dinner, anticipating his return from work.

Abubakar was tired. He had been away from his family for four days and they had sailed through a storm coming home, making sailing treacherous. He was soaked to the bone and every limb felt heavy. They safely moored the boat and Abubakar gathered his things together.

As he walked home, his spirits lifted. He had missed Amira and Bay and was looking forward to seeing them both. He smiled at the thought of giving them the gifts he had found on his journey.

As he opened the door into the kitchen, Amira turned, a smile of greeting on her face, and Bay shouted, 'Da Da home,' from the table where he was banging a wooden spoon. 'Bay helping Mama,' he said happily.

'I can see that,' said Abubakar, and chuckling, he kissed his son on the top of his head inhaling his baby smell.

He gathered Amira into an embrace, noting the dark circles under her eyes. He kissed her gently on the mouth. 'I'm so glad you're home,' she said.

'Me too,' said Abubakar, and Amira sighed into another kiss. He gently rubbed her swollen belly. 'How are you feeling?' he said. She smiled tiredly at him. 'Another nightmare?' he said, and as Amira nodded, her smile wobbled, and tears quickly filled her eyes and started to roll down her cheeks. Abubakar gathered her close. He hated seeing her upset.

With a last hiccup, Amira stopped crying. Abubakar gave her another squeeze. 'Why don't you wash your face, and I will finish serving dinner.' He watched Amira leave the room.

'Why Mama sad?' asked Bay.

'Mama had a bad dream,' said Abubakar, ruffling his son's hair. 'But she is alright now,' he said.

Bay nodded his head. He banged the wooden spoon on the table. 'Bad dream gone,' he said, nodding his head, and with one pudgy hand, he swept it onto the floor. Abubakar nodded his head at his son and spooned some stew into the bowl in front of him.

When Amira came back in, she looked a bit calmer. Abubakar placed a steaming bowl of stew in front of her with some freshly baked bread. 'It smells delicious as always,' he said. He smiled at her encouragingly and she spooned some stew to her mouth. Her stomach growled reminding her that not only she but also their unborn baby was hungry. Amira pushed her worries aside for now and enjoyed her meal, listening to Bay chatter away to his father about his day.

'Mama bad dream gone,' said Bay with a vigorous nod, again banging his spoon, stew, and all on the table to show how he had squashed the bad dream.

Laughing, Amira said, 'Yes Bay. Thank you, sweetie.' With the tension melting away for now, she enjoyed the sound of her family around her, feeling comforted.

After they had eaten and bathed an unwilling Bay, Amira and Abubakar told him a bedtime story and soon he was snoring softly. They both kissed him on the cheek and left him to sleep. Amira showed Abubakar what she had written that day in the garden. He was quiet as he read through everything she had written. 'We have some time at least,' he said, holding up a piece of parchment.

At Amira's confused look he pointed to a line she had written, 'You mention your babies.'

'I don't even remember writing that,' Amira said, taking the parchment again and rereading the line.

'It's possible you have more clues than you realise,' he said. 'I think it's a good idea to write down anything you can remember,' said Abubakar.

'And anything that comes after this too,' said Amira. 'It made me feel a little bit more in control.'

'I wish I had been here,' said Abubakar, gently cupping Amira's face in the palms of his hands and wiping a tear away from her cheek with his thumb.

She hadn't even realised that she had been crying. 'Me too,' whispered Amira. Abubakar gently kissed her on her lips and then lifted her onto his lap so that he could cuddle her.

'Shall we sit in the garden?' he said. Smiling, Amira nodded her head, and, to her delight, he stood up with her still in his arms and walked out to her haven. He knew how the garden relaxed her. He was always so thoughtful.

Abubakar sat outside with Amira in his arms looking up at the moon and stars. He sent a prayer up to the gods to protect his precious family. His heart would break if he lost her. She was so brave his wife. She didn't think so, but he saw how she pushed her worries aside to protect Bay. He saw her strength and kindness when helping friends and clients with her healing potions. It took strength to see what she saw in her visions. Yes, she was strong his wife and he loved her with all his heart.

He needed to make a plan to protect her when he was away. Sometimes he could be gone for weeks, and he couldn't leave her unprotected. She had another month before their baby was due. He also needed to find out where Baahir was. He hadn't visited or communicated with his parents in some time but was never truly far away.

He came out of his musing, and looking down at Amira in his arms, he realised she had fallen asleep. He sat for a little while longer sketching a plan in his head. Satisfied he had somewhere to start, he stood up slowly, careful not to jostle Amira. He carried her in gently and laid her on their bed. He undressed quickly and got in, holding her in his arms. He covered them both over and, with Amira in his arms, fell asleep.

Chapter 25 – Baahir

Baahir was going to propose today. He had it all worked out. He had been wooing Bennu for a few months now. Bennu owned the local tavern The White Feather, which was a bedrock for secrets and lies. Perfect for him to collect or even sell secrets for the right price, which aided his business.

He had been paying Bennu compliments and sending her presents. What she lacked in beauty she definitely made up for with her other assets (the main one being the tavern itself which was a goldmine for the reasons previously stated). He had treated her like a maiden, which he was more than certain she wasn't. She seemed to melt in his presence. Yes, he had primed her well.

He went to her mid-morning with flowers and a bauble and knocked on her private door. She didn't have a lot of free time but what she did have she spent in her own quarters. She opened the door having just awoken from sleep. She was wearing her nightshift with a shawl over her shoulders. *She had ample curves; he would have no problem bedding her,* he thought.

Her eyes opened wide at the sight of the flowers. 'Good morning beautiful,' said Baahir, holding the flowers towards her.

'Thank you, Baahir,' said Bennu taking the flowers. She stood aside for him to enter. Her rooms were small, but she kept them clean, as she did the tavern. She had worked as housekeeper for a high-born family at one point. He suspected that she had bought the tavern after being paid off to leave. He wasn't sure of the reason; it could have been theft, or he even suspected that she had been caught with the man of the house by the lady of the house.

He never asked and she never said. He sat down at a scarred but clean table and Bennu bustled around putting the flowers in water. She seemed uneasy but he wasn't sure. *Surely, she would feel privileged at his proposal. How could she not?* he thought.

So, Baahir took a deep breath and said 'Bennu, we have been seeing each other for a while now. I think you know how dear you have become to me. Would you consent to be my wife?' With a flourish, he opened the box with the ring inside. Bennu stared at him in shock for a moment.

The word *wife* seemed to hang in the air. Bennu assessed Baahir sitting in front of her. He was always washed and dressed in clothes made from the finest material. She knew he had been attentive for a reason, and she knew that reason had more to do with the tavern than her. She had heard lots of rumours of Baahir and his business dealings. She hadn't heard any stories of him with other women, she thought, which was a plus. Most rumours of the unsavoury kind always made it to her ears, whether she wanted to hear them or not. It kind of went with the job.

She did not love him; she wasn't even sure she liked him. He was handsome enough, she thought. The truth was, she wanted a child and felt that her time was running out. There had been no other interest for a long while now; well, not the sort of interest she wanted when it came from one of her drunken regulars. Baahir would treat her well she believed. He worked away a lot and she didn't believe he would need much of her time and attention.

She had been in love once. Oh, she had been a silly girl believing the beautiful words told to her by her master's brother. She had believed he thought she was beautiful and that he wanted to take her away from her life of drudgery. She had been such a fool. He had flattered her right into his bed, and she had been caught leaving his room by her mistress.

Her *suitor* had been betrothed, and they had wanted to join their great families and become more powerful. She had been dismissed the next day.

'I'm sorry Bennu. I like you; you are a good worker and kind-hearted. I should have protected you better,' said her mistress sadly. 'I can't let you stay. We can't have a scandal.' She handed Bennu a bundle of food and a purse of coins. 'If there are any repercussions,' she said, looking at Bennu's middle, 'send word to me.' And with that, Bennu was out on the street.

Crying, Bennu gathered her meagre possessions together and left. *Where would she go?* Her mother had put her into service at a young age and she had been working for the same family for years. There was no way her mother would take her in. She would know of her disgrace as soon as she walked through the door. She wandered the streets all day trying to think of a solution. Tired, she collapsed onto the grass and cried at the thought of her fate.

This was where Dalila found her. Dalila owned the local tavern with her husband. Her children lived in the city, and she didn't get to see them or her grandchildren as much as she would like. She had a great big heart and always had plenty of love to spare for waifs and strays. She helped Bennu up and led her to her quarters and made her some tea. Her husband popped his head into the kitchen briefly and chuckled at his wife. 'Another stray,' he said, not unkindly. 'My wife has a heart too big for her chest,' he said to Bennu. 'Welcome.' And he went back to attend the bar.

'Why don't you tell Dalila all about it?' And between sobs, the whole sorry tale came out.

Clucking like a mother hen, Dalila mopped up her tears and gave her a motherly hug. 'You are welcome to stay with us while you work out what to do,' said Dalila.

Bennu was humbled by her kindness and said, 'Thank you.'

'Not at all,' said Dalila. 'We have our daughter's room sitting empty. I hate an empty room, don't you? It's so sad. I think my daughter's clothes should fit you too. She left them behind when she married her husband and I hate to throw good clothes out. That's if you don't mind of course.'

Dalila didn't pause for breath and didn't seem to require a response at that moment, so while she was chattering away, she got Bennu settled in her daughter's room.

When Bennu was alone, she opened the parcel of food that her mistress had given her. There was more than enough for three people so she decided she would share it with Dalila. When she opened the purse strings and emptied the contents into her palm, she gasped at the number of coins gleaming in the light. Her mistress had been generous indeed. Bennu safely tucked the coins away. She would hold onto them until she figured out where she would go.

There was a gentle knock on the door, and at her answer, Dalila popped her head around the door. 'I thought you might be hungry,' she said as she entered the room with a tray.

'Thank you. You have been very kind,' said Bennu.

Dalila waved off her thank you and popped the tray on a small table in the room. 'Why don't you eat this and have a sleep. You look worn out. We can talk further tomorrow.' She patted Bennu on the arm and left her alone.

Bennu ate the contents of the tray and drank the tea that Dalila had brought her. Realising how tired she was, she undressed. She washed her face with the water that Dalila had thoughtfully prepared for her, and she fell asleep as soon as her head hit the pillow.

The next morning, Bennu awoke to the sounds of people going about their day. She wasn't used to sleeping so late as she normally arose early to go about her duties and was surprised that nobody had come in to fetch her. As she sat up, the memories of yesterday returned and tears of hurt and humiliation consumed her once more. She was sure that her heart had broken in two.

There was a gentle knock on the door and, wiping her eyes, she called out. 'Hello.'

'Why don't you come down for some breakfast?' said Dalila. Bennu brightened with the remembered kindness of Dalila yesterday. A complete stranger had shown her more kindness than she had experienced from her own mother. She quickly got up, washed, and put on the clothes that Dalila had kindly set out the night before.

She entered the kitchen to wonderful smells and her stomach grumbled in anticipation. 'Dig in,' said Dalila. Dalila watched as Bennu filled her plate and stomach, a motherly smile on her face. 'I like to see my cooking enjoyed,' she said.

Bennu looked up, a flush of embarrassment colouring her face. 'I didn't realise how hungry I was. I'm sorry, I usually have better manners than that,' she said sheepishly.

'Nonsense, you don't stand on ceremony with family.'

Bennu's heart lifted at the kindness of this women in front of her. She was offering to take her into her family and to give her a home. 'You don't even know me,' said Bennu. 'Are you sure?' Dalila looked at Bennu for a moment. It was if she was looking right into the heart of her and, without realising it, Bennu held her breath.

Coming to a decision, Dalila nodded her head. 'I could do with some help around here if you would like. I'm not as young as I was,' she said. Bennu doubted that Dalila had any trouble with the tavern and was as robust as any person half her age, but she recognised a kind offer when she saw one. She wasn't one to be idle and had worked from a young age. This way she would feel like she was working for her keep.

'Thank you,' she said to Dalila. Again, Dalila waved her thank you away with her hand as if she were swatting a bothersome fly.

Bennu fell into the rhythm of the tavern quickly and found she quite enjoyed the work. Dalila and her husband made sure things didn't get too rowdy and the locals had too much respect for them to cause trouble. Bennu woke up one morning just over a month after Dalila and her husband had taken her in, rushed to the chamber pot, and retched. She washed and swilled her mouth and went down to breakfast as always.

When she entered the kitchen, instead of the smell of breakfast making her mouth water as usual, she felt decidedly nauseous. Dalila looked up in greeting, but the smile on her face froze at the look on Bennu's face. 'Are you ok sweets?' she said. 'You look decidedly green.'

'It must be something I ate, or maybe I've picked up a sickness bug off one of the regulars. I'm sure I'll feel better later,' said Bennu, trying to smile to reassure Dalila.

Dalila looked at her knowingly but simply nodded her head in agreement. She gave her a piece of dry bread. 'Just try a little, it will help,' she said. Bennu nibbled the bread, and her stomach settled a little.

Unfortunately, the sickness returned repeatedly throughout the day. It also carried on into the next morning and the morning after that.

The morning after that, Dalila thought enough was enough. She gently knocked on Bennu's bedroom door and listened for her voice to come in. It sounded weak to her ears. She opened the door and found Bennu lying on her bed looking worn out. Bennu opened her eyes as Dalila entered. Dalila passed her a washcloth to cool her face. 'You know what's wrong with me, don't you?' she said.

'Don't you?' asked Dalila gently.

Bennu nodded her head, 'I think I'm pregnant,' she sobbed.

Dalila hugged Bennu gently as she cried. 'What am I going to do?' she sobbed.

'You are going to do the same as you are already doing. You will stay here for as long as you want to. I can help you with the babe. Everything will work out; you are not alone. Now, wash your face and come downstairs and we will try and get some food into you.' Smiling, Dalila left the room. She was looking forward to having a babe among them. It had been a long time since she had held her grandchildren in her arms, and she missed them greatly.

Thankfully, after a couple more weeks, the worst of the morning sickness abated, and Bennu felt much better as her energy returned.

As her pregnancy started to show, she didn't go to the markets as much for fear that word would get back to her old mistress. She had made her peace with the past and was excited to meet the new life growing inside of her and felt fiercely protective. She was afraid of what her mistress would do if she found out.

Another month passed and Bennu started to relax. As she came downstairs from an afternoon nap, there was a knock on the front door to their lodgings. She automatically opened the door and, to her shock, standing in front of her was her old mistress. Bennu froze. 'So, it is true,' said her ex-mistress. Bennu felt like fainting and took a step back, not sure what to do. Thankfully, just at that moment, the connecting door to the inn opened and Dalila walked in.

Dalila looked first at Bennu and then at the elegant lady in the doorway. Assessing the situation, she rightly figured based on the look on Bennu's face that this was the mistress who she had kept house for. 'Why don't we all sit down?' she said, taking Bennu's arm gently and leading her to the kitchen table. Bennu sunk gratefully into the chair and looked at Dalila stricken. She couldn't get the words past the fear clogging her throat.

The elegant lady followed them into the kitchen and, to her credit, sat down without looking down her nose at the surroundings. Dalila looked around her kitchen trying to see it through the elegant lady's eyes and decided she didn't care what the lady thought. Yes, her kitchen was worn but it was also clean. Her home was lived in and had seen much love and laughter.

'I see you know my daughter-in-law, so you must be the *lady* she worked for,' said Dalila. The lady didn't miss the inflection on the word *lady*. She felt the reprimand clearly from the women in front of her and liked her for it. She was right of course; Bennu should have been safe in her employ. 'Bennu is giving me the wonderful gift of another grandchild. My son is very excited about being a father. He is away at the moment working so that he can send money home, so Bennu is staying with me while she has the babe.' Dalila happily chatted over Bennu's gasp, which, smart girl that she was, she covered up with a cough.

Dalila looked up from pouring drinks to look squarely at the lady who was looking at her intently. Dalila hadn't discussed with Bennu a backup story should this lady turn up, but she was determined to protect her and had devised a plan from the start. Bennu took a moment but, after squaring her shoulders, she also looked up at her ex-mistress. Dalila wanted to cheer at her bravery.

The lady nodded her head. Whether she believed them or not, she had obviously decided this was for the best. She touched Bennu's hand gently and then, standing, she placed a purse of coins in the middle of the table and turned to leave.

Bennu wanted to push it away, to refuse the money. She wanted to shout that she didn't need paying to keep quiet, that she didn't want anything to do with the father so why would she cause trouble.

She was about to stand and say just that when she felt Dalila's hand on her shoulder. 'That is very generous of you, my lady,' said Dalila.

The lady paused at the door and turned around. 'I am truly sorry that I did not protect you better in my home. I wanted you to know that and to know that I have missed you. I am glad that you have found a good home.' Before Bennu could say anything else, she left.

After the lady had gone, Bennu looked at Dalila. 'I didn't know you had a son,' said Bennu with a knowing smile on her face.

'No?' said Dalila. 'Didn't I mention him before? Strange that.' She squeezed Bennu's hand. 'I hope you didn't mind. I have already been telling that story to anyone impertinent enough to ask. It seemed the most plausible.'

'How can I ever repay you?' said Bennu. 'First you save me, and then my babe.' She got up and kissed Dalila on the cheek. 'I love you. You have been more of a mother to me than my own ever was. Thank you.'

'It was nothing,' Dalila said, gruffly trying to wave off the moment, but Bennu saw the tears in her eyes before she turned away.

Dalila helped Bennu prepare her room for the arrival of the babe. She cleared an area where Bennu could bathe and dress the babe, and her husband moved in a chair for her to sit and feed and rock the babe to sleep. He was just as excited as Dalila and kept turning up with toys or clothing that he happened to see at the market for a bargain price. For the first time in her life, Bennu was truly happy. She had a family and a home where she was loved.

Seven months into her pregnancy, Bennu woke up with a scream. Severe pain slashed across her stomach, and she felt nauseous. She was frightened. It was too early for the babe to come. When another jolt of pain slashed through her middle, Bennu screamed for Dalila and then doubled over gasping for breath.

Dalila came bursting through the door and for once she looked ruffled and fearful. Seeing Bennu doubled over in pain, she sent her husband to get the healer. Pain ripped through her heart for little Bennu. She had seen this before and was fearful that Bennu was going to lose the babe. She squared her shoulders. She couldn't let Bennu see her fear; she needed her now.

Dalila rushed to Bennu and put her arm around her, lending her some of her strength. 'I'm here Bennu, you are not alone, I am here.'

Bennu looked up at Dalila, tears streaming down her face. 'Something is wrong, it hurts so much. The babe?'

'The healer is coming,' said Dalila, squeezing Bennu's hand in comfort.

Ramla arrived. She had been visiting family in the area when Dalila's husband had come to fetch her. Dalila waited with her husband in the kitchen. A short time later they heard the door of Bennu's room open and close as Ramla came into the room. She shook her head sadly and Dalila burst into tears in her husband's arms. He had never seen her like this before; she was always such a strong woman and to see her like this broke his heart. 'Bennu?' he asked.

'She is resting comfortably,' said Ramla. 'She should rest for a couple of days. I will come and see her again tomorrow.'

'I need to speak to you about arrangements,' said Ramla gently. Dalila looked to her husband as she composed herself. He nodded and Dalila went to see Bennu while he made the arrangements for their special little bundle.

Bennu losing her baby made Dalila miss her grandchildren more and more, so her husband suggested that they sell the tavern and move closer to their family. They begged Bennu to go with them. 'A fresh start for you Bennu. Away from the sadness. Please come,' said Dalila.

Smiling at Dalila, Bennu shook her head. 'Yes, there has been sadness recently,' said Bennu. 'But there are lots of happy memories here too. This is the only home I have ever really had. It feels a part of me and working at the tavern gives me a purpose. I can't imagine living anywhere else. I have been thinking and I would like to buy the tavern from you. I have the money my ex-mistress gave me,' she said and named a price.

'That is more than the tavern is worth,' said Dalila. 'But if it's really what you want to do. Will it be enough for you?' said Dalila.

'I don't know what the future holds,' said Bennu. 'Maybe I will meet someone and have a babe. It's not something I can even contemplate right now.' She looked around the tavern imagining herself as the proprietor and it was a nice feeling. 'I've never had anything that was all mine before.'

Dalila saw the look on Bennu's face and knew she had made up her mind. 'The White Feather will be in good hands,' said Dalila. 'I'm not taking all your money. You have more than enough to buy The White Feather and still have plenty over. Promise me you will visit us though. I will miss you so much,' said Dalila, giving her a hug.

'Yes, and you must come visit me too.' They hugged again.

A week later, with their cart laden with the possessions they had decided to take with them, they were ready to go. There were more hugs and tears and, as they were about to go, Dalila looked down at Bennu. 'You may not have come to me as a babe, but you will always be my daughter Bennu,' and she blew her a kiss as they departed. Bennu waved until she could no longer see the cart. She turned towards The White Feather with tears running down her face but a smile on her lips. She would miss them dearly, but she also felt a new chapter of her life beginning.

Bennu shrugged off the memories. Baahir wanted an answer and she had made her decision. She liked her life and was content overall, but lately, the thoughts of settling down and having a family of her own had been making themselves known more and more to the point she could no longer push them away. 'Yes Baahir,' she said, 'I will marry you.'

The breath Baahir had been holding whooshed out of him. 'Splendid,' he said. He couldn't believe he had doubted she would say yes. It was him asking after all and it wasn't like she had men lining up waiting for her.

He took the ring out of the box with a flourish and lifted her hand off the table. 'Wait,' she said. He paused, confused. 'Before you do that, there are some ground rules.' Something flickered in his eyes and then, smiling, he looked at her with what she could only decide was respect. He let go of her hand and sat back in his seat.

'I want a babe,' she said. 'I don't love you and I know that you don't love me. I know why you are marrying me so please understand I am not a foolish girl looking for love from you. I make a good living and that will continue. The tavern and all its dealings remain mine. How you make your living is up to you and I wish no part of it. You can come and go as you wish.' She paused for breath. 'Do you agree to these terms?'

Baahir paused, absorbing all she had said. He had underestimated her it would seem. He respected her for speaking out and felt they would rub along very nicely indeed. He couldn't have chosen a better wife. Baahir looked at Bennu with new eyes and respect. She worked hard and had pride in The White Feather. It was well known and even more popular than before she had taken it over. She would be a good mother to any children they had. He nodded his head. Smiling, she lifted her hand, and he placed the ring on her finger.

Chapter 26 – Amira

Amira walked into her parents' home and found her mother Anipe sitting at a kitchen table, a letter in front of her. 'Everything OK?' she asked her mother who seemed to be sitting very still and in shock.

Anipe looked up at Amira. Picking up the letter, she passed it to Amira. 'Your brother is getting married,' she said. 'He wants us to go to his wedding.' Amira skimmed through the missive. Baahir was to be married to Bennu in a few weeks' time. They were invited to attend the ceremony and a small party at The White Feather after.

'What are you going to do?' said Amira.

Anipe shook her head slowly. 'I don't know.' They exchanged a knowing look. There was still so much pain and distrust when it came to Baahir. 'He is still my son,' said Anipe sadly.

'Well, I for one have to admit my interest is piqued. I would like to meet the woman to take on Baahir,' said Amira, trying for levity.

Smiling, Anipe nodded her head. 'As would I. I don't know whether to hug her and welcome her to the family, tell her to run as fast as she can, or lock away any valuables,' she finished sadly. Mother and daughter hugged.

'Let's have some tea and we can discuss it with Abubakar and your father later. Pass my grandson here. I need a cuddle.' She kissed and cuddled Bay prompting his squeals of delight. Amira had baked her mother's favourite sweets, so they took them outside and sat and enjoyed the sun.

Chapter 27 – Amira

Despite Baniti and Abubakar's better judgment, they decided to attend Baahir's wedding for Anipe's sake. They knew that Baahir had been using their names to enable his business dealing, without their permission. As long as his dealings didn't reflect badly on their business, they would say nothing, but they would keep a close eye on him. Their close business contacts knew and kept them appraised of any business dealings offered by Baahir. So far, none of their business contacts had dealt with him and all his dealings so far had seemed above board, as much as they could tell.

Baahir wasn't stupid and knew not to try and do business with the same people as his father. His business contacts were a little less flush in the purse as it were, but it suited his needs for now. He knew how loyal his father's and Khnurn's business contacts were and had no wish to try and compete in that echelon of business, although he believed he belonged there himself.

When they had discussed wedding plans, Bennu had asked him who he was inviting from his family. He didn't want to explain the reason for their estrangement, so he wrote a letter to invite them. He would blame their absence on his father's health if needed.

Bennu had invited Dalila and her husband, children, and grandchildren and was very excited they were coming. She had also invited a few neighbours and close friends. Bennu and her friends had decorated The White Feather for the occasion, and it was fragrant with flowers.

Bennu was to get ready at home and Baahir at a neighbour's. He would then meet her at the small chapel where they were to be married by Ramla their local priestess. She had nearly refused when she found out that it was Baahir who was getting married, knowing of the rift with Anipe and her family, but she remembered the younger Bennu and couldn't refuse.

Baahir was waiting at the small chapel for Bennu when he spotted his mother coming towards him. Further behind her he could see his father, his sister Amira, her husband Abubakar, and their two children, their little boy Bay, now two and a half, and their six-month-old baby girl Jendayi who was in her daddy's arms.

Baahir's heart clenched. For the first time in his life, he wanted something that wasn't all about him. He wanted someone to care for. He wanted a family of his own. He wondered what it would be like to hold his baby son or daughter in his arms. His partnership with Bennu now had new meaning.

'I didn't think you would come,' he said to them at large.

'I wanted to,' said Anipe. He nodded his head and gave the rest of the family a tentative smile. His mother hugged him and then stepped back to stand with the others to await his bride. He watched his father put his arm around his mother protectively.

At the sound of footsteps, Baahir took his gaze off his family to see Bennu walking towards him. She was the most beautiful woman he had ever seen. How was it he had never noticed how beautiful and graceful she was before? The truth was, he never looked past himself. He didn't see her because he was only ever considering what he wanted. She had on a simple gown of ivory. In her hands she held a small bouquet of flowers, and the same flowers weaved through her hair, which fell loosely behind her back.

Baahir felt a protective feeling come over him he hadn't felt since he was a child and Amira had come along. Unfortunately, jealousy had grown until it replaced the protective feeling altogether. Now, looking at Bennu, he wanted to do better, be a better man than he was now. Maybe Bennu could help him. 'You look beautiful,' he said to her. Surprise flitted across her face before it softened into a smile.

'You look very handsome too,' she said. Baahir felt himself puff up with pride and he took her hand in his to lead her to introduce her to his family.

After the ceremony, the small group walked back to The White Feather for the festivities. Bennu took to Baahir's family straight away and they in turn liked her very much. She introduced her new mother- in-law and father-in-law to Dalila. She introduced Dalila as her second mother, to Dalila's delight. She left them talking for a little while and walked over to speak to Amira who was bouncing her little girl on her hip and trying to control an adorable little boy.

'Can I help?' she said, smiling at Amira.

'Cake?' said Bay, looking up at her with hope in his eyes.

'Cake it is,' said Bennu laughing. She looked at Amira for permission and, at her smile and nod, led the little boy inside so that she could cut him a piece of wedding cake.

'Pretty,' he said, pointing to the flowers in Bennu's hair while trying to put as much cake into his mouth as possible.

'Slowly,' she said to Bay. 'It isn't going anywhere.'

'You are good with him,' said a voice behind her. She turned to see Anipe smiling at her and Bay.

'G'mar,' said Bay around his mouthful of cake. Bennu wiped some frosting off his chin.

'He is adorable,' said Bennu.

Anipe joined her and they chatted for a while, and then she took Bay to his father. Anipe saw Baahir standing by himself and went over to him with a drink. 'Thank you,' said Baahir, taking the drink from his mother.

'She is lovely,' said Anipe. Baahir followed his mother's gaze to where Bennu was laughing with one of her friends. She looked younger today, carefree. He felt pride swell in his chest.

'She deserves better than me,' he said, surprising himself.

'You will look after her won't you Baahir?' said Anipe. There was worry in her voice.

'She makes me want to be a better man,' said Baahir. 'I think she can make me a better man.'

Anipe looked from Bennu to her son. She saw a difference in him and prayed what he said was true. 'Try and be happy son. Try and be content. I see sadness behind her eyes. She deserves to be happy. She will be a good wife and mother, I think. I hope that you can deserve her.' She turned to her son, took his hands, and looked deep into his eyes. 'I think this is your last chance son. A fresh start. Leave the past behind you and truly embrace a life that will make you happy. If you don't, all you will have is regret and, I suspect, ruin.' Letting go of his hands, she turned to walk away.

Baahir watched Bennu as she mingled among her guests making sure everyone had food and drinks and were enjoying themselves. He watched her with the children; she seemed to light from within. She would make a good mother. He wanted to give her that chance. For the first time he wanted to look after someone else. He wanted to put her needs before his. It was a new and humbling feeling. She deserved better than him he knew, but she had married him, and he would be a better person for her, if it killed him trying.

When all the guests had left, he found Bennu tidying up. He took her hand to stop her. 'We can do that in the morning,' he said. Smiling, she nodded her head, and they sat down together for a quiet drink.

'What a beautiful day,' she said, stifling a yawn. 'You have such a lovely family and I feel so blessed to have all our loved ones together under one roof. Family,' she sighed, 'there is nothing more important than family.'

'Bennu,' he said, holding her hand. 'I know I agreed to the terms of our marriage.' Stricken, Bennu tried to pull her hands away. 'No, I'm not going back on them,' said Baahir, soothing Bennu with his words. 'What I'm trying to say is, I want to try and have the real thing.' Bennu looked at him, assessing. 'I know I asked you for the wrong reasons, but seeing you today, I feel as if I saw you truly for the first time. I want a real family. I don't know if I am capable of real love, but I want to try, with you. I have been a selfish man all my life, I see that now, and maybe that is ingrained so deep I am incapable of change, but you make me want to try. What do you think?'

Bennu sat for what felt like hours assessing his sincerity. He couldn't blame her he supposed, but still, it stung a little.

Did he mean it? she thought. *Was he sincere?* She had learned to read people well over the years working at the tavern. After the trouble her foolish and youthful heart had gotten her into, she promised she would never be taken in by a man again. She recognised the signs when Baahir was lying. In fact, he wasn't as good a liar as he thought he was. Even when he was being nice, he couldn't hide the greed, dislike, or jealousy. They always seemed to be there in his eyes.

She didn't judge; many of her patrons had secrets or past indiscretions they chose to forget. She thought maybe Baahir had had a bad upbringing and that was why he was like he was. But after meeting his parents and sister, she was even more confused as to how and why he had turned out the way he had. They seemed kind and hardworking people. His sister was a seer and a healer, and Bannu had heard wonderful stories of her kindness and the help she had given to the community far and wide.

She believed that Baahir believed his words. He wanted to be a better man. Maybe marrying her and having a family would be the making of him. Maybe he would fall into old habits. She couldn't be sure. She could see the intent in his eyes and, oh, how she wanted a family of her own.

'I would like that,' she said. 'But let me make this clear. If you step out of line. If you fall back on old ways and hurt me or any children, we are lucky enough to have. If you put any of us in danger, you walk away. You leave us and never come back.'

Baahir listened to Bennu's terms. He was confident that if he put his mind to it, he could change. He could be happy and make Bennu and their children proud of him. He nodded his head. He held her right hand across the table. He took her left hand and placed it across his heart. 'I promise you that I will try, until I take my last breath, to deserve you.' And with this pledge, he placed a kiss in the centre of her palm.

Looking around at the happy mess in The White Feather, Bennu felt the possibility of their next chapter. She stood, still holding Baahir's hand, and led him to their quarters. 'You have pledged to me with your words. Now for the rest.' And Baahir finished his pledge with his body, heart, and soul. As they fell asleep, he prayed to the gods for the strength to change.

Chapter 28 – Emma and Kyle

Kyle and Emma both dated other people during their time at university. They even introduced said boyfriend or girlfriend to each other. Kyle even liked some of the men that Emma dated and vice versa. However, they wouldn't admit it to themselves at the time, but their respective partners never seemed to match up to how they felt about each other.

They supported each other through their breakups over beer, pizza, and ice cream, and Kyle would send Emma flowers and chocolates to cheer her up. They wanted to be able to bash their exes, to say that they were better off and that they didn't deserve to be with Emma or Kyle, but the truth was that, deep down, they knew the reason why they didn't work out, so it wouldn't be fair for them to do that.

It was during one of these breakups, with Emma wiping her tears and eating ice cream, when Emma, shaking her head, said, 'I can't do this anymore.'

Kyle's heart stuttered. 'What do you mean?'

'Us,' said Emma. 'I love our friendship and I know if things were different, if we were in the same country,' she said with a sad smile, 'that this would be different.' She took a deep breath, organising her thoughts. 'I think we should give ourselves that chance. Maybe if we have some distance for a while.' Distance. Kyle felt the irony of the word. He couldn't seem to get the words past the lump in his throat to tell her she was wrong. But she wasn't wrong, and she deserved to be happy, he wanted that for her. 'Goodbye Kyle, I love you,' said Emma as she burst into tears and disconnected their internet call.

Kyle sat back, shocked. What had just happened? His heart felt tight in his chest, and he felt moisture in his eyes. This felt worse than any breakup he had had with a girlfriend. He had just lost his best friend and he felt as if a part of his heart had been ripped out and that he would never recover. He shook his head at his dramatic thoughts. He had always thought of himself as pragmatic and not prone to drama of any kind. He needed to fix this, but how?

The next month was the most miserable of his life. It was supposed to be a time for celebration. He had just received his university results and had outdone himself, getting a first. His thoughts strayed to his future, and he had to admit that all his plans had always featured Emma in them. His heart always knew where they were headed even if they didn't.

His first instinct was to call Emma, but she ignored all of his calls. He had tried to respect her decision but had only lasted an hour before trying to ring her. His call went to voicemail, so he left a message and sent her a text message, but still no reply.

He had had an interview with the head of the university last week and had been offered a teaching position at the university. Outside term time he was free to attend archaeological digs, as he was keen to keep his practical experience up to date. It was a great opportunity, but the truth was, he was torn.

He wanted a life with Emma. He could see a home with her, children. Should he take the job or try and get a job in America? Was that what she wanted too? He really needed to talk with her but how could he if she wouldn't take his calls?

Then he had a frightening thought. *What if she had already met someone? Someone she could see her future with. See herself having a family with. What if he was too late?* He got up from his desk and paced around his room.

Chapter 29 – Emma

Emma was having the dream again. It always started the same way. Her eyes felt heavy, and it was an effort to keep them open. She wished Abubakar was there; she prayed he would find her in time but feared he would not.

She prayed for her children and that they would be ok without her. Her body felt lethargic, and everything felt like it was slowing down. She must fight it; she must stay awake. She would fetch some water she decided, but she couldn't move. Her legs and arms felt as if they were weighted down by an invisible force.

Her nightmare was coming true. Her brother had managed to drug her somehow. She thought she had been so vigilant when he was there earlier. She had prepared all the food and drink. How and when had he done this to her? And the biggest question of all, why?

She wanted to scream out for help but there was no one there. Abubakar wouldn't be home until morning and the children were at a neighbour's.

She heard a noise coming from the other room. Her heart lifted; maybe it was Abubakar home early and all was saved. Relief flooded her body. But it wasn't Abubakar who walked into the bedroom. The figure looming over her wasn't her husband's loving face but the face of her brother Baahir.

'It's OK,' he said. 'Close your eyes. It will just be like going to sleep; no pain, I promise.'

She tried to hold on for Abubakar. She tried to hold on for the children, but whatever Baahir had given her was too strong. With her last ounce of will taken by the potion and with a single tear running down her face, her eyes closed of their own will. Was this the end? *I love you*, was her last thought before the darkness swallowed her whole.

Emma woke screaming Amira's name and burst into tears. She got up and fetched a glass of water. She sat on the couch with a throw around her shoulders in the comforting yellow light of the table lamp.

She had been having the same nightmare for a week. The same torture night after night. In the light of the lamp, she could feel her fear ebbing away. *Amira*, she thought, *what happened to you?* For she was sure that she was dreaming of Amira and that the horrible nightmare she was living each night Amira was about to live for real. She felt so helpless. How could she warn her friend?

As much as they had a connection, whenever she linked with Amira it was by chance and she never had any control over the meeting. She believed that it was instigated by Amira, but the conversation had never come up.

She desperately wanted to call and talk to Kyle, but the way she had left things, she didn't feel it was right. She knew nobody else would understand as he would, but she also knew how much she had hurt him and herself.

She checked the time and calculated it would be eight o'clock in the morning in the UK and Kyle was probably already up and about. Making a decision, she reached for her phone with shaking hands and dialled his number.

He picked up on the third ring. 'Em?' he said. 'I'm so glad you called. I've been thinking long and hard about what you said. I've tried to call you. I've booked a flight for tomorrow to come and see you. It's the earliest I could get. I'm not ready to let this end. Emma, I love you and I'm willing to find a way to make this work if you are.' So much had been going through Kyle's head the last couple of weeks. Should he let Emma go? Should he let her find her own life without him? But the thought made him miserable. The truth was, he wanted his life with her. If not now because of their commitments, then later. He had no inclination to date anyone else. He just wanted to be with Emma.

Emma burst into tears on the other end of the phone. She too had been miserable the last couple of weeks. She had thought if she distanced herself from Kyle she could move on, but the truth was she loved him. She couldn't imagine having a life with anyone else. Her love for him wasn't the only thing drawing them together. Amira also drew them together and her dreams not only affected her, they affected Kyle too. She realised that now.

'Emma, what is it? Emma, tell me, please don't cry.' Kyle wished that he could hold Emma in his arms and comfort her.

Emma managed to get herself under control. 'I love you too,' she said. 'We can talk when you come. I want to make this work too. There is something else I need to tell you,' said Emma, filling Kyle in on her dreams.

Emma described the dream to him, and he listened carefully, taking in all that she said. He then asked question and she tried to recall as many details as possible, from how dark it was and how warm it was to any items in the room that stood out. It was like he was creating a map in his head. For what, neither of them knew. Yet!

'We need to warn her. You need to warn her,' said Emma.

'I need the amulet,' said Kyle. 'Is it at the museum or with the owner?'

'It's at the museum,' said Emma. 'It arrived yesterday and goes on display in a couple of days. I'll make the arrangements with mom,' said Emma, marvelling at the timing.

'I've got an early flight in the morning so should be with you around six. If you can make the arrangements at the museum for the next day, we can try and warn Amira.'

'I'm glad you called,' said Kyle gently.

'Me too,' said Emma. 'I'm sorry for hurting you. For hurting us both.'

'We'll figure this out,' said Kyle. 'I'm willing to wait if you are. Life is all about timing. We'll talk more tomorrow.'

'Send me your flight details. I'll pick you up from the airport,' said Emma. 'Kyle?'

'Yes?'

'I love you.'

'I love you too Em. See you tomorrow.'

Chapter 30 – Kyle

When Kyle held the amulet in his hand, he had the same tingling feeling that he had had both times before. This time he felt a little more prepared.

The tingling started in his hand radiating from the amulet, although the amulet itself felt cold in his palm. As the tingling feeling spread through his body, he looked at Emma. She smiled encouragingly at him. 'Good luck,' she said. He closed his eyes as the feeling intensified like having pins and needles over his entire body. Then, to Emma's eyes, he went completely still as if in a trance. His breathing slowed, and his body went stiff. Under his closed eyelids, Kyle saw stars before he felt an overwhelming falling feeling.

When Amira walked into her bedroom, she found a man standing there. She felt a scream building in her throat when he turned around and held out his hand. 'Don't be afraid,' he said, 'I won't hurt you.' In that instant she recognised him, and her fear melted away.

'I'm not afraid,' she said, 'I know you.' Relief swept through Kyle. He had been worried she would scream, and he had no idea how he could possibly explain his appearance to her husband or anyone else who walked in. Amira smiled at him, 'My Truth Seeker,' she said. True, he was a few years older from when he visited her the second time, but she recognised him.

Kyle didn't know how long he had; he didn't want to be blunt, but he needed to warn her. 'I have something urgent I need to tell you. I'm guessing from our previous visit that my time is limited, so here goes.

Your dream that you have about your brother,' he paused, trying to find the right words.

'How do you? ... Emma, of course.' Amira paled and fear and sorrow passed across her face.

He reached out and held her hand and, as if drawing strength from his touch, she looked him in the eyes and squared her shoulders.

'Where is Abubakar?' Kyle asked.

'He is away; he doesn't come home until tomorrow morning,' said Amira. Fear filled Kyle's heart; surely, he hadn't come all this way for nothing.

'Can you get a message to him somehow?' he asked.

Amira thought, 'His ship is due in the morning. I could send a note.

There is more,' said Amira. 'My brother is here. He turned up out of the blue. He said he needs to speak to me about something personal tonight and asked me to send the children to a neighbour. I was just coming to pack some things for the children. I don't understand; I thought he had changed. He has his family now and he seemed happy. Bennu said recently she was worried about him and that he had been acting secretively, but why would he do this? He could just ask us for help.'

Kyle was thinking fast. He couldn't believe that he had been brought through time. He still couldn't believe this was actually happening and that he wasn't dreaming; maybe he was, but it felt real. He couldn't believe this would have happened only for him to fail.

'I don't know,' said Kyle. 'All I know is that Emma has been having the same dream, the same nightmare, for a couple of weeks and she is worried. She asked me to come and warn you.' Kyle quickly described the dream to Amira. Nodding her head, with tears in her eyes, Amira confirmed it was the same dream that she had been having over the last couple of weeks.

'Have you eaten or drunk anything tonight that you haven't prepared?' said Kyle.

Amira thought for a moment and then shook her head. Her dream came back to her, the feeling of heaviness taking over her body, how tired she felt, and how she struggled to keep her eyes open. 'You think he means to drug me?'

'I think so yes. Emma remembers her eyes closing completely but also remembers being carried before she completely loses consciousness. We don't think it ends here. We need a plan and fast. We need to get a letter to your husband. We need to get help!'

'I will send my son Bay. He is wiser than his years and sensible. He has an older friend, and I am sure he will go with him. It is a lot to ask of my baby,' Amira said sadly.

'What about a neighbour? Can someone else help if Abubakar cannot get here in time?'

Amira nodded. 'Bay's friend has an older brother; I don't know if he is home or working away though.'

'Will your brother take the children to your neighbour, or will he let you take them?' said Kyle.

'No, I will take them. I don't want to scare my babies,' said Amira.

'I know, but I don't have any other ideas. Do you?' Amira sadly shook her head. Kyle continued, 'I think we may need to ask more of him. I think he will need to watch and follow Baahir. We believe whatever he intends, it doesn't end here.'

Amira nodded her head. She went over to the desk and wrote a quick note. She showed it to Kyle, and he was surprised to see it was written in English. He knew that Amira could speak very good English from his previous visit but was surprised that she could write it too. 'My secret weapon,' said Amira. 'Thanks to Chione, Emma's mom, I can both speak and write in English. She taught Emma and Emma taught me. I later taught my husband at his request and our children. It is out secret language,' Amira said proudly.

Kyle smiled back feeling proud of her and her family as though the achievement was his own. He sensed that his time was nearly up. He wanted to stay, to do more, but he didn't know how.

'It's OK,' Amira said gently. 'You have done all you can. The rest is left up to the gods, but I thank them for sending you to me. 'Goodbye my Truth Seeker. Say hello to My Heart when you are back with her again.' She took the amulet from his hand. 'Thank you for returning my necklace.'

Kyle felt himself falling once more. 'Good luck,' he said.

He was back in the room sitting at a table with the amulet in his hand. It was the same room at the museum. Emma took it from him gently and placed it back in its cushioned case.

He was out of breath; his skin was clammy, and he was shaking all over. Emma took one look at him and led him to the restroom. He splashed water on his face, and she got him a glass of water.

Emma patiently waited while he recovered. His face was pale, and his hands were still shaking. When he had recovered some, he filled her in on what had happened. 'Do you think we helped?' said Emma.

'I don't know. I hope so.'

Chapter 31 – Amira

When Kyle had gone, Amira went over to the herb chest in her bedroom. Remembering what Kyle had said and the effects she had felt in her dream, she mixed herself a potion and drank it quickly. Not knowing what her brother planned, she wasn't sure if it would work but maybe it would buy her some time.

Her brother was waiting for her when she came out of her bedroom. He looked at her curiously. 'I heard you talking in that strange way of yours. Is everything ok?'

Amira smiled at her brother. 'I was talking to my Truth Seeker,' she said. Baahir had heard her use this term before and just nodded his head condescendingly.

'I will take the children to Keira's. I won't be long.' She gathered her three children together along with some things they would need for the night and led them out of the door.

She could just run she thought. Hide and find Abubakar in the morning, but she sensed her brother's desperation and feared more for her children and husband than for herself. She must let this play out and have faith. Faith in her protector, her brave Truth Seeker, and Her Heart, and for the gods watching over her.

She filled Bay in on the way to Keira's. He listened intently and nodded to confirm he understood what she had told him. 'Come with us,' said Bay, clinging to his mother's hand. She hugged him and his brother and sister tightly.

'I love you and I am so proud of you all. Remember that.' She kissed them all in turn and ushered them into Keira's house. She was afraid to be too long in case Baahir got suspicious. 'Look after my babies,' she said to Keira. She hugged her startled friend and left.

Bay watched as his mother headed back towards their home. He wanted to follow her, to protect her, but his uncle was bigger than him. He needed his father.

He was worried for his mother, but he would do what she asked. He explained everything to his friend Lateef and his mother Keira. Keira, looking concerned, called in her eldest son Sethos who was three years older at fifteen. He usually worked with his father who worked for Bay's father but had stayed home this weekend because he was unwell. She instructed Sethos to watch Bay's house, and if Baahir left with Amira, to follow and report back. 'Be careful,' she said to her son. He nodded and quickly left by the back door so that he wouldn't be noticed. He would circle back around until he had a clear view of the house and be unobserved.

Bay and Lateef left shortly after that; with the note from his mother safely tucked away, they ran as fast as they possibly could, faster than either of them had run before. They knew these streets and had run through them many times. They knew every shortcut and made full use of them now. Thankfully, there was a full moon tonight and the silvery light lit their way like a beacon.

Bay ran with his heart pounding and a stitch forming in his side. He knew time was of the essence. He was so frightened, but with Lateef by his side, he felt braver. He needed to get to his father. His ship was due to dock tonight, but his father wouldn't disembark until tomorrow morning.

He feared that would be too late. He saw the fear in his mother's eyes, which she tried to hide from them. He felt her goodbye in her hug and kiss. What was his uncle going to do?

Chapter 32 – Amira

After hugging the children and leaving Bay with the letter and instructions, Amira reluctantly returned to their house. Her feet were dragging and her heart sinking, not sure what her fate was. She had to believe that Abubakar would make it in time. That Baahir didn't really mean her harm.

When Amira entered the house, Baahir was sitting at the kitchen table where she had left him. She tried to muster a smile so he wouldn't be suspicious. She only hoped the potion she had taken before dropping the children off with Keira would help counteract whatever he had given her, for she knew how smart her brother was and she had no doubt that he had drugged her.

She should have been more careful. After having the dreams for a while, she had thought she was prepared, but when nothing had happened, the more time that went by, she had relaxed. She thought Baahir had settled down and that he was happy. She thought the threat had gone away. She admonished herself again, but there was nothing more she could do now. She believed that whatever Baahir had planned, if he thought she knew anything about it, he would not be happy. He prided himself on how smart he was and would hate if anyone even had an inkling of his plans.

So, she would play along as she had no choice. She feared if she said anything that he would hurt Abubakar or, even worse, the children. She smiled and offered Baahir a drink. To her surprise, Baahir yawned and said it grew late and that Amira looked tired. He said what he had to say could wait and suggested they talk another time and then took his leave.

Amira felt relieved. Maybe the Truth Seeker was wrong, maybe she was wrong, and it wasn't tonight. Maybe there was a reprieve after all. Amira thought of fetching the children back but realised that she did in fact feel tired. Not wanting to disturb them in case they had already gone to sleep, she decided to go to bed.

Preparing herself for bed and yawning what felt like every ten seconds, the blood faded from Amira's face and the relief went in a flash. She realised that her tiredness wasn't natural and was progressing with some speed. With fear of falling on the floor and knocking herself out or injuring herself, she took two steps towards the bed and collapsed onto it. She should run for help, but her energy was fading fast and her body becoming so heavy she couldn't lift her limbs.

She was too late. Baahir had already set his plan in motion. She only wished she knew what that plan was.

Chapter 33 – Baahir

Baahir walked just out of view of Amira and Abubakar's home and waited. What was he doing? he thought. This was stupid. He should go right back there now and tell Amira what he had done. He would wait for Abubakar to come home and ask for his help.

But it was too late, he thought in horror. He had already slipped the drug into her water when she was talking to the children. Judging how tired she had looked when he left, he calculated that it wouldn't be long before the drug took effect. He didn't have the antidote with him, and the priest had been very specific on how long it would need to take effect and how long he had to get her to the antidote. No, it was best to follow through. He would only scare Amira more trying to explain to her now. So, he would wait and return at the right time.

While he sat by the riverbank in the quiet listening to the insects and local animals either settling in from the day or waking up for the night, he thought to himself, *Day has handed over to night and the gods said to each other, 'I have taken care of the day for you. You take care of the night.'*

His mind flashed back to two nights before and the circumstance that brought him to his desperate and ridiculous plan.

He had been sitting at his desk, his head in his hands. He was aboard his ship. He was tired to the bone and wanted to go home. But more than that, he felt despair in every cell of his body.

What was he going to do?

He had been away from home for a month and desperately wanted to see Bennu and their son, but he couldn't go home yet. He had to make a plan. He had to figure out what to do.

He had sunk every penny he had, and, God forgive him, he had even put the tavern on the line. He was that sure his new venture would work and that they would be rich enough to retire. Bennu would never have to know.

Not only had he used every penny of his own money but also every penny of his three investors. Two of these he wasn't worried about. They would give him time to repay. He was worried about Abasi and his men though. They would want to be paid on time and, if not, they were quite happy for you to repay in other ways. Less savoury ways. Baahir shivered with fear at the thought.

His cargo hold was half full of stock. Stock that was ruined. Stock he couldn't sell. He had merchants lined up along the Nile River. He had already sold his stock before he had collected it, and now, he was ruined.

When he had arrived to collect his stock, the merchant had happily opened containers to show him vegetables, herbs, and gemstones. He had laid out colourful and shimmering fabrics. Satisfied, Baahir had paid him the money and ordered his men to load his cargo.

With a satisfied smile on his face, they set sail for home. He would make his stops along the way, collect his money, and have a day or two in each place for food and drink. He was at his third stop sitting in a tavern when one of his men burst through the door. Shocked, Baahir waved him over. His men never bothered him when he was off ship. He preferred it that way.

What he whispered in his ear shocked him so much he threw too much money on the table to pay for his meal and, gathering his things, ran with him back to his ship. His men confirmed the truth. The top of each container did in fact have fresh veg or fruit, beautiful silk, or gleaming gemstones, but strip the top layer away and the food was rotten, the gemstones worthless, and the fabrics ruined.

He had sent some of his men back to the merchant. They had returned this morning to say there was no sign of him. He had left with the money and there was no trace behind him. Baahir was ruined. Bennu could lose the tavern and she would never forgive him. How could he go home now? How would he live with the shame?

His day was about to get a lot worse. One of his men was strong-armed into his room and his shout of 'I said I don't want to be disturbed!' caught in his suddenly dry throat. For there, holding one of his men, was Abasi. Here was a man who wasn't frightened to get his hands dirty. He twisted his arm until he cried out in pain, then pushed him towards one of his men who flanked him on each side.

'Go look and take him with you,' he said in a frighteningly calm voice. His men left him and Baahir alone. Abasi watched him with cold calculating eyes making him uncomfortable. He liked making people feel uncomfortable. It made him feel powerful.

Baahir opened his mouth to speak. He didn't know why because he had no idea what he was going to say. Abasi stopped him by putting his finger to his own lips in a shushing motion. Then he waited.

It seemed like forever they were that way. Him at his desk and Abasi filling his doorway. He could feel his heart beating in his chest and his blood humming in his ears. He could feel a trickle of sweat run down his forehead but didn't dare move a muscle to wipe it away. Fear pooled in his belly.

One of Abasi's men came back and, with a nod of his head to Abasi, left again. Abasi looked back at Baahir. 'So, it is true,' he said. 'How much do you have left?' he said, referring to the money he had given him. Baahir reached into his desk draw and withdrew the money he had taken from the merchants that he had already left the goods with.

'I have to give that back,' he said, trying to square his shoulders. 'It is the right thing to do.'

'And how do you expect to pay me?' said Abasi with a raised eyebrow.

'Please do tell. I am very interested to hear what you have to say.'

Baahir swallowed the lump in his throat, desperate to come up with a plan. 'What, the famous Baahir lost for words? Where are all your pretty words and promises now Baahir?'

'The White Feather is yours,' said Baahir desperately.

Abasi leaned his head to one side.

'We both know that won't cover it all,' said Abasi. 'It is a start. Why don't you try again?' he said in a silken voice.

Baahir racked his brain. He tried to think out of his acquaintances who would be able to produce the money quickly. There were a couple he knew could, but he had burnt those bridges a long time ago.

Abasi sneered and looked at Baahir like a bug he would like to squash under his foot. 'Out of ideas?' Abasi rubbed his chin. 'I'll take your ship and the tavern. That should cover half of what you owe me. You have a week to produce the rest. I think that is rather generous of me, don't you?

In the meantime, why don't you pay a visit to that brother-in-law of yours and his beautiful wife? I've always fancied spending some time with her,' he said with a cruel look on his face. 'Almost as much as your wife.

We will be watching Baahir. You have one week to produce our money, or we may pay a visit to that lovely wife of yours. Such a fine-looking woman, it would be a shame if she were to have an accident. It would also be a shame if that lovely sister of yours was to … shall I say, disappear.' Baahir stood quickly in protest, his chair hitting the floor. Before he could take a step towards Abasi, he pulled a knife from nowhere and sliced off a piece of Bahir's hair. He grabbed Baahir's wrist and, holding his hand to the desk, he quickly brought the knife down and stabbed the desk between two fingers. He stepped away from Baahir leaving the knife in place and drew another from his waistband in case Baahir had any ideas.

Holding up the piece of hair, he threatened. 'Next time I will take more than a piece of your hair. Don't underestimate me Baahir and don't try to double-cross me. Nobody survives that.' He left and Baahir carefully moved his hand away from the knife sticking out of the top of his desk. Picking up his chair, his shaking legs gave way and he collapsed into it.

He needed a plan, and he needed one fast. He couldn't just ask Abubakar for help. Although things had been better since he had married Bennu as she had a close relationship with his family, they still distrusted him. No, he needed leverage. Just enough for Abubakar to help him with no questions asked. He had put everyone in danger. He had to make it right. He looked down at the desk at the lock of his hair, left as a warning.

Back by the river, he looked up to the heavens. 'God,' he prayed, 'what do I do now?' He waited. No answer. Wearily, he got to his feet. It was time.

He entered quietly, listening for any movement. Deciding all was safe, he made his way to the bedroom where he could see a soft glow of light. Amira was lying on the bed, and he could see she was fighting to stay awake. There was no use, he thought, the potion of deadly nightshade would be too strong to withstand and soon she would be taken over by its power.

He stood over her and could see the fear and questions in her eyes. He didn't have time to explain. Time was of the essence, so he simply said. 'It's OK, close your eyes, it will just be like going to sleep, no pain, I promise.' As Amira succumbed to the potion, her eyes closed, and her face and body went slack. Baahir quickly went to the kitchen and scattered the contents from the table onto the floor and tipped the chair over, making it look like there was a struggle. He would come back in the morning to warn them about Abasi but see he was too late. He could see that Abasi's men had gotten there before him and taken her as he had threatened. He would return her once Baahir paid him the money he owed him.

Yes, it was better this way, he thought. He could keep Amira safe from harm of Abasi and get Abubakar's help without question. *Better him take Amira than Abasi,* he thought with a shudder. He would bring her back safely and unharmed. *Yes, this was the better plan,* he told himself.

Baahir made his way back to the bedroom. Amira looked so tiny and helpless lying there on the bed. *I will keep you safe,* he thought. He quickly looked outside to see if anyone was about.

Making his way back inside, he gently wrapped Amira in a blanket. Checking outside once more, he was relieved to see that nobody was around. He carried Amira out and placed her in the cart and covered her over so that she was no longer visible. He needed to get her to the priest. He was to revive Amira and keep her out of sight while he returned for Abubakar's help.

Time was of the essence when using deadly nightshade and he didn't have much more time, but he believed he had planned it down to the minute detail. He jumped into the cart and took the reins to get the horses moving. He shook the reins but one of the horses refused to move. Cursing under his breathe, he shook the reins again but there was still no movement from the horse.

In his haste to get to the house that night he hadn't checked the horse's hooves. It had lost a shoe on the way over and appeared to be lame. In anger and fear, he kicked the horse, which made it rear and shy away with a cry. He immediately regretted his show of anger and released the horse. He prayed one horse would be fast enough and got back in the cart and was off.

He flogged the horse trying to make up the time he had lost. When they arrived at the funeral home, the horse was bloody, out of breath, and covered in sweat. He threw the reins on the ground and carried Amira to the back door of the funeral home where he was met by two burly men. They took Amira none too gently from his arms. 'You know what to do,' he said. They nodded. 'I will be back in the morning.'

Baahir left the funeral home on foot. He saw a dirty boy looking at the horse and cart and threw him some money. 'Take care of them and they are yours,' he said, walking away.

He spent the night on his ship. Tomorrow he would visit and check on Amira and then go see Abubakar. The quicker he could get this over with the better. Amira had said he was due to dock tonight so he should be home in the morning.

The next day Baahir stood outside Abubakar and Amira's home. He couldn't move; couldn't bring himself to push the door that was already ajar, further opening up to and admitting to Abubakar what had happened. What he had done. *It's the least you can do,* he thought. Squaring his shoulders and taking a deep breath he walked in.

The cups and bowls were still on the floor as well as the chair. Abubakar must just have arrived back himself. He was standing at the table reading a letter. Baahir's step faltered, his heart pounding in his chest, fear swirling like a thousand beetles moving around in his belly.

Abubakar turned towards him with fear and confusion on his face. 'What have you done?' said Abubakar, walking menacingly towards him. They were of equal height, but Abubakar was broader than Baahir, and with the anger he could see in his eyes, Baahir took an involuntary step backwards. 'What have you done?' Abubakar said. The fear and confusion had been replaced with controlled fury. Baahir could see fear mixed in with the fury flit across his face like a shadow.

He knows, thought Baahir, *but how*? Abubakar passed him the letter. It was written in his sister's hand. *Last night*, he wondered. *When? How?*

The writing was shaky as if written in a hurry and under great emotion. Some of the ink had smeared from tears.

The letter was written in strange symbols he didn't recognise but he sensed what the contents meant, and he could clearly see his name.

'Don't make me ask you again,' said Abubakar with such controlled fury in his voice that Baahir took another involuntary step back.

He contemplated making a break for it but knew he wouldn't get far.

How did it all go so wrong and how could he tell Abubakar?

Thinking back to his morning with sadness, he couldn't undo what he had done but maybe he could make amends somehow.

'Where ... is ... she?' Abubakar enunciated each word slowly, his patience wearing thin. Baahir froze, he didn't know how to tell him. His throat clogged up and he couldn't get the words out. The words that would destroy Abubakar and any hopes he had of receiving his help.

When Baahir had woken up that morning, he had been sure all would be well. He would get Abubakar's help. He would return

Amira unharmed and go home to Bennu. He would retire from shipping and live a good life with her. It was too late for that now. He had lost Bennu forever and destroyed Abubakar's life too.

He had arrived at the funeral home where he had left Amira the night before, ready to tell all and beg for her forgiveness. Beg her for her help so he could put things right. He had knocked on the door impatiently, waiting to gain entrance. The door opened slowly and one of the men from the previous night peered out at him. Recognising him, he stepped back and allowed him access.

Baahir went in quickly, wanting to make sure Amira was all right. He entered the main room, but she was nowhere to be seen. 'Where is she?' he demanded of one of the solemn men standing to attention to one side. He nodded to the table. Baahir looked at the small figure on the table covered in salt (this was the first part of the mummification process to remove the moisture from the body).

Confused, Baahir looked from the figure back to the man. 'No, where is my sister?' Baahir said again to the man, getting irritated. Again, the man nodded to the figure on the table. One of the priests took that moment to enter the room seeing the exchange. He had not liked Baahir when he had first met him. He was a man who collected information and wasn't afraid to call in a favour when he needed it. Baahir listened well and collected secrets like others collected jewels. The priest was not a man to be trifled with, but he had a secret and somehow Baahir had found it out. To his surprise, he had kept his secret. When he came to him for help, looking desperate, he promised to keep Amira safe. 'Where is my sister?' Baahir demanded again. 'This fool keeps directing me to this unfortunate soul.'

The priest nodded at the other man to dismiss him. 'I am sorry Baahir,' said the Priest. 'He is correct, that is your sister.' Baahir looked at him in horror.

'What? How? What did you do?' he spluttered, going purple in the face.

'Not me,' the priest shook his head sadly. 'We could not awaken her; you took too long. We tried everything we know to revive her, but we couldn't. I am so sorry.' The priest walked towards his sister, turning his back on him to give him a chance to absorb the information.

Open-mouthed, he stared between the priest and his sister's still form, shaking his head, refusing to believe what the priest was telling him. The enormity of what he had done finally hit him. He crumbled to the ground, overcome with remorse and guilt. 'I am sorry,' the priest said. 'We didn't feel it right to leave her, she deserved more respect than that. So, we began the process.' Baahir nodded his head.

After what seemed like an age, he got up off the cold hard floor and paid the priest to take care of his sister. He didn't have much money left but he owed her that. He asked them to paint the name Panya (mouse) on her finished sarcophagus. It was a nickname he had had for her when they were children. She was always so quiet and timid, and he had called her his little mouse. 'I will protect you little mouse,' he would say when they were little.

Looking at the priest, he tried to convey that this was not what he wanted, not his intention at all. This isn't what he wanted; his poor beautiful sister was no more. What had he done? How would he ever forgive himself? She was kind and gentle and offered much more to the world than he did. She was happy and he had taken that away from her. She looked so small lying there, so small and lost.

She had always been kind to him even though for the most part he hadn't deserved it. Even though he was always jealous of her and sometimes spiteful, she always looked past that to the insecure person within. Always tried to see the best in him, even sticking up for him more than he deserved. He had thought that no one would ever love him like that. He was very rarely kind to her. She had been of no use to him as a child, so he mostly ignored her. As she had grown older, so had her beauty. He'd seen how Abubakar looked at her; now she was useful to him. He encouraged Abubakar's affection for her; he even anticipated their marriage. He thought their marriage would give him control over Abubakar. He hadn't expected them to fall in love. The control that he thought he would have was gone. He could see that her allegiance would always lie with her husband.

Then he met Bennu. Bennu and Amira helped to mend their family.

'Forgive me sister,' he said out loud.

Abubakar was still staring at him intently and he remembered he was waiting for an answer.

How could he tell him? He was going to kill him, he knew it. 'She's dead,' he said opening his eyes.

At Abubakar's stricken face, he closed them again. 'It was an accident,' he implored. Opening them again. 'I didn't mean for this to happen. You have to believe me.' He braced himself for the attack he was sure would come, but Abubakar stood very still. He shook his head trying to deny what he was hearing.

'How?' his voice came out strangled.

'I needed to keep her safe and I needed your help,' said Baahir.

'Why didn't you just ask me for help?' said Abubakar.

It sounded so simple. Why hadn't he? Because he hadn't believed that he would give his help freely. 'I had a plan,' he explained.

'You drugged her. How is that keeping her safe? What else did you do?' He took a menacing step towards Baahir now. Baahir took a step back, cringing at his own cowardice.

'Nothing, I promise. It was an accident. She ... succumbed to the potion. It wasn't supposed to happen. She was to be revived when we were away from here.' To his great embarrassment Baahir crumbled to the ground in tears. But were they tears of remorse or fear for himself? Abubakar wasn't sure.

Abubakar had never felt such anger and fear in his life. Fear for Amira and their children, and fear for what he might actually do to Baahir if he stayed in his presence much longer. He had never wanted to kill a man with his own bare hands before. He practically shook with the restraint he had on his temper.

'Get out,' he said, desperately trying to calm himself. To hold himself back. 'NOW!' he shouted, pushed past his endurance. He had no time for Baahir's cowardice and pretend show of remorse. Baahir flinched. He seemed to collect himself and ran out of the door.

Chapter 34 – Baahir

Bennu opened the door in the morning to ready the inn for the day, only to find Baahir asleep on the doorstep. He had been gone for over a month, supposedly on business, but he had been acting strangely for a few months before that.

She called his name and shook his shoulder. He awoke with a start. 'You look terrible,' Bennu said worriedly. Baahir always prided himself on being clean and tidy. He was covered in dirt and dishevelled. He had at least a week's worth of facial hair and he always liked to be clean shaven. He had lost weight and had dark shadows under his eyes. 'Why didn't you let yourself in?' said Bennu.

Baahir looked into the eyes of the only person beside their son that he had ever loved. In fact, he had never known love until he met her. He had fought against his parents' and his sister's love and refused to open his heart to them in return. He had thought he was incapable of love. He couldn't bear to see that love disappear from her eyes.

At the look on Baahir's face, Bennu took a step back. 'What's wrong Baahir? What has happened?'

To Bennu's dismay, Baahir crumbled in front of her eyes. She had never seen him cry before and this was so much more.

She pulled him up by his arms and dragged him inside. 'Baahir, tell me. You are frightening me.'

Bennu tried to comfort him, but he wouldn't let her. She sat down at the kitchen table and waited for Baahir to get himself under control.

Once Baahir had recovered some semblance of control, the first thing he said was 'I love you, Bennu. Please forgive me. I couldn't bear it if you hated me too.'

Bennu was about to speak but Baahir squeezed her hand to stop her. 'I'm so sorry sweetheart. Please let me get this out and then I will leave.' And Baahir told all. Bennu to her credit waited until he had finished.

Baahir finally plucked up the courage to look her in the eyes. She had her hands clasped tightly over her mouth and tears streamed down her face.

Shaking her head, she got up from the table and paced around the kitchen. She looked at the stranger at the table feeling as if she didn't know him at all. She knew he had his faults but never thought he could cause so much pain.

'You could have just asked Abubakar for help,' said Bennu. Baahir nodded his head. 'I realised that too late,' whispered Baahir.

'Oh, Baahir how could you? To Amira. Oh, my gods, to Abubakar and their babies. Why Baahir? Why?' she finished in a ragged breath.

'We would have lost everything. You would have lost the inn,' said Baahir, hanging his head in shame.

'It isn't yours to lose,' said Bennu.

'They wouldn't care,' said Baahir.

'Why Baahir? How did you come to this? I thought that was all in the past. We were happy. I thought you were content?' Bennu sat back at the table feeling her legs wobbling from all the emotions coursing through her.

'I wanted to give you more. I borrowed money, but the stock was bad. I was cheated and I felt like I was drowning. It was too late to tell you then. I couldn't admit that I had failed you.

Abasi threatened you. He threatened Amira.' Baahir dragged his hand over his tired face.

'Oh Baahir, can't you see I had more than I ever thought I could have. I had a home, a family. I have been happier than I ever thought possible. I didn't need more. I'm sorry that it wasn't enough for you,' she sighed sadly.

'Did you tell Abubakar about Abasi. About where Amira is?'

'He told me to get out. He told me never to go back,' said Baahir. He felt defeated. He had lost everything precious to him and he only had himself to blame.

'You can't leave it like this,' said Bennu, fresh tears trailing down her face. 'I'll go.'

'I can't ask for his help now,' said Baahir.

'You won't be here when we get back will you?'

Baahir shook his head. 'It isn't safe for you if I stay. I don't think you should come back here either.'

Bennu shook her head, fresh tears streaming down her face. 'It's my home.'

'I know sweetheart and I'm so sorry, but it might not be safe for you both.'

Bennu nodded her head in defeat. 'We'll go and stay with Delila. She has been asking me to for a while. I will lock up the inn until I know what to do with it and make arrangements for it to be watched and for our things to be sent on.'

'I'll send you word when I have settled and send money when I can. Can I say goodbye to Ammon?' said Baahir, referring to their son.

'He's going to miss you so much. You are a good father Baahir, and you have been a good husband.'

'I love you, Bennu. I'm so sorry I did this to us. Sorrier than I can ever say.' He got up from the table and kissed her on the forehead.

Bennu heard him go upstairs and talk to their son. She waited at the table until she heard him come back down the stairs and heard the front door open and shut. He was gone. Bennu wanted to fall apart. She took a deep breath and pushed herself up from the kitchen table.

She packed what she and Ammon would need for their journey to see Abubakar. She had no idea what she was going to say to him when she got there. She only hoped he would listen.

She wrote a letter to her friends next door and asked them to keep an eye on the inn for her. She told them she was going away for a few days and would write to them again soon. She took one last sad look around her home and, picking up Ammon, made her way outside with their packs. She posted the note through her neighbours' door and made her way out of town.

It took two days to get to Abubakar's home. She and Ammon were exhausted when they got there. She prayed that Abubakar wouldn't turn them away.

As she approached the door, she knew something was off. There was no answer at her knock. She peered in the window, but the house was empty.

'They've gone,' shouted a neighbour. 'Terribly sad business. He took the children, hired a nanny, and left to start afresh. Amira will be sorely missed around here. Such a kind and gentle young woman. Terrible business,' said the neighbour, wiping her eyes.

She looked at Bennu more closely. 'You're their sister-in-law, aren't you? I recognise you from your visits. You and the wee one look exhausted. You poor dears. You come in now and rest with me a little while. I have a spare room now my daughter has got married, so there is room for you both to rest.' She grabbed Bennu as her legs gave way. 'Let me take the baby for you and let's get you both inside.'

Bennu thanked the kind neighbour and followed her inside. Her home was welcoming and smelt of fresh bread. She showed Bennu to a bedroom and put a now sleeping Ammon in the middle of the bed. 'You lie down there for a bit, and I'll bring something to drink and eat.'

The neighbour didn't know where Abubakar had taken the children. Bennu stayed in her care for a couple of days before they both felt ready for their onward journey to Delila's.

She was sad to not be able to go back to the inn, but Baahir was right, it wasn't safe for them now. She knew that Delila would welcome them both with open arms. She didn't know whether she would see Baahir again, but she felt positive that she could create a new beginning for her and their son.

Chapter 35 – Emma and Kyle

Emma awoke with a start. Bright morning light shone beneath the curtains. It was light and the alarm had not gone off. A flash of memories of the night before flashed through her mind and a smile crept across her face, quickly to be removed again when the panicky thought that had woken her up re-entered her mind.

They were late; they had a flight to catch this morning. Kyle was taking her home to meet his parents and brothers in person; she had only spoken to them over the internet before. She felt a slight tremble in the pit of her stomach at the thought. She reached over to gently shake Kyle awake. She wondered if he was a morning person, and whether he woke easily or if he was a deep sleeper. *I suppose these are the sort of things you find out from experience*, she thought. She was more than ready to learn all those things about him.

Last night had just felt right. She had never felt so comfortable with anyone. She had always hoped that when she met the man that she was destined to spend her life with, that it would just feel right. Last night was the first night they had made love. He had undressed her so gently, looking at her as if she were the most beautiful woman in the world. She had never felt that before. Never been looked at like that before. Men had always made her feel like a giant, ungainly and awkward, not womanly at all. But last night as Kyle undressed her, she felt womanly and almost dainty. Just the thought brought a chuckle.

She wondered whether she should put the coffee on before waking him. She gently shook him again, hoping that would be enough to wake him up. He stirred and opened his eyes. Very sleepy eyes, the most beautiful sky blue. Then he smiled at her and reached up to draw her head down to his to place a sleepy kiss to her lips. 'Good morning,' he said, smiling again, his voice gravelly from sleep. He was the sexiest sleepy man she had ever seen, and she wanted nothing more than to sink back down into the kiss and spend the rest of the day in bed with him.

Watching her emotions as they passed across her face, he smiled and reached for her again. With resignation, she pulled back slightly. 'We are late for our flight; we really need to get moving.' He came awake in an instant and reached for his watch on the bedside cabinet. Confirming the time, he leapt out of bed and started grabbing his clothes from the floor where they had been discarded the night before. She was transfixed by the sight of his very cute, very naked bottom. Sensing her eyes on him and recognising that she hadn't also jumped up and started scrambling around for her clothes, he looked over his shoulder at her. With a cheeky smile on his face, he raised one eyebrow and drawled, 'I thought we were late.'

Laughing, Emma jumped up and started to gather her clothes together too. 'You go use the bathroom first. I'll put some coffee on.'

Kyle made his way to the bathroom, shouting over his shoulder, 'Thank God we have already packed.' On their way back from the restaurant last night they had stopped off at his hotel and collected his things. Emma had also packed the day before so that her luggage was ready to go. Putting on her dressing gown, she made her way downstairs to the kitchen to put on some coffee. She got down two travel mugs to fill to take with them. They would have to get some breakfast on the way.

While Kyle was in the bathroom, she quickly checked around her home to make sure everything was secure. She loved her home. Cosy and full of colour, her home was her haven, and she always felt like it gave her a warm hug as she came through the door. No matter what sort of day she had had, no matter the weather outside, she felt herself relax as soon as she stepped through the door.

She imagined what it would look like mixed with items of Kyle's and hummed to herself while she waited for the coffee. There was plenty of time for all that, but they had wanted this for so long she didn't want to waste another minute and she believed that he felt the same way.

They had been talking about a possible future for so long and had already decided on this visit that she would go back to England with Kyle to meet his family. He had been offered a teaching position at Cambridge University and she had been offered a coveted position at the museum with her mom. They were still countries apart, but she felt that they had a future together, the timing just wasn't right yet. He always enjoyed his visits with her and, although he loved England and always referred to himself as a 'Little Englander,' he said he would be happy to join her there. Last night just seemed like the icing on the cake and the beginning of their next chapter together.

'What are you thinking so seriously about?' Startled, Emma looked up to find Kyle smiling at her from the kitchen doorway.

'You,' was her shy reply. 'Our future together, here, you and me.'

He smiled at her with his love shining in his eyes. 'I like that idea,' he said, drawing her into a searing kiss.

When they came up for air, Emma passed him the coffee mug. 'You fill and I will get dressed.'

While Emma was getting dressed, her mind wandered to thoughts of meeting Kyle's family. She shook off her nerves and laughed at herself for being silly. They had already spoken so many times she already loved them like family. They were a part of Kyle, and she could always feel the love and closeness he had with his family. It was one of the things that had attracted her to him in the first place. No matter what was going on in his life, he always said that if you were going to worry, then make it about what really mattered, like family.

She was looking forward to seeing more of England. She couldn't believe that she hadn't visited them before. She felt selfish now; she hadn't realised how she had encouraged him to come to her and should have offered to visit him instead. She was staying for a couple of weeks to spend time with his family and to take day trips with Kyle. Kyle encouraged her to pack for all weathers just in case. It was currently summer in England, but it was known for its unpredictability when it came to the weather.

Emma realised she had paused in getting dressed as her thoughts took over. There was a gentle knock on the door and Kyle popped his head in. 'Are you ok?' he said. Emma nodded her head but must not have been that convincing. Kyle smiled and came into the room. Taking Emma into a hug, he said, 'You will be fine. They already love you and you have spoken to Mum lots of times. She will make you feel welcome, I promise.' Emma sunk into Kyle's embrace, enjoying soaking up his strength. He kissed her on the lips. 'Finish getting dressed,' he said. 'The taxi will be here in ten minutes to take us to the airport.'

With the tingle of his kiss still on her lips, she quickly finished getting dressed. She had just finished when she heard the beep from downstairs to indicate the arrival of the taxi. She rushed out of the bedroom. Kyle was at the door with their luggage. 'I'll take these downstairs while you lock up,' he said.

They bundled their luggage into the taxi and settled in the backseat. Kyle squeezed Emma's hand and she felt the tension melt away. He could always do that for her. In a situation where she would normally be feeling stressed and worked up, he would take her hand and she would feel calmer.

The taxi driver dropped them off at the airport for their flight and they checked in. They had some time before their flight so decided to have some breakfast while they waited. During their flight they talked about where they would go during Emma's visit.

When they landed, Kyle collected the car that his parents had kindly left at the airport for them to use. He dropped Emma at the hotel first so that she could freshen up. It had been a long flight, so they decided to eat in the hotel and then get some sleep. Kyle was staying with his parents during their visit so he would drop off his luggage and check in with his parents before meeting her back in the bar.

The meal at the hotel was lovely but soon tiredness took over and they decided it was time to call it a night. 'Stay,' said Emma.

'Are you sure?' said Kyle. Emma nodded her head, and they headed up to her room. He texted his parents to let them know he would see them in the morning. They both undressed, gratefully sank into the comfortable bed, and promptly fell asleep.

Emma woke to an unfamiliar room and blinked trying to recall where she was. Kyle stirred next to her, and she remembered they were in a hotel in Coventry, England. 'Morning,' he said, smiling. She felt her heart lift. He leaned over and kissed her gently on the mouth. He then got up and filled the small kettle in the bathroom and put it on to boil.

While it was boiling, he texted his parents to say they would meet up with them in the afternoon. 'I think we deserve a lazy morning.' He made himself a cup of tea and Emma a cup of coffee and climbed back into bed.

He finished his tea quickly and Emma was still finishing her cup of coffee when he started to nibble on her neck. Sighing, Emma put her cup on the bedside cabinet and sunk into Kyle's embrace.

When they came up for air, they ordered room service. 'They said it will be about an hour,' said Kyle when he put the receiver down. 'Fancy joining me in the shower?' Kyle with a lop-sided grin said. Smiling, Emma decided that was a very good idea indeed.

Chapter 36 – Kyle

Kyle opened his inbox to the most extraordinary email from the University of Entdekung in Germany. He had to speak to Emma about it, but first he needed to do some digging. He knew the name but wanted to refresh himself.

It was announced in July 2018 that evidence of an ancient Egyptian funeral home was discovered at an archaeological dig in Saqqara. It was discovered deep beneath the sands on the bank of the Nile less than 20 miles south of Cairo, in a sprawling necropolis known as "The City of the Dead". It is believed that there are many more overlooked by excavators whose aim it was to get to the tombs beneath.

Hussein began the excavation at Saqqara in 2016 searching for tombs dating to around 600 bc. Hussein and his team made the discovery while investigating an area that was last examined in the late 1800s.

Kyle was reading through the National Geographic website looking at all the fascinating photos of what Hussein and his team had discovered.

After this shocking discovery, other sites had been re-examined. The email was from a professor who had excavated one of these sites. *What on earth could he possibly want with him? Not just him, but Emma too,* Kyle thought?

He contacted Emma that night on *Google Duo* and asked her if she knew of Hussein and the discovery of the ancient Egyptian funeral home by him and his team. Emma did and they discussed this for a while until he realised that they had digressed, and he brought himself back to the reason for his call. The cryptic email…

'I will read it to you,' said Kyle.

'Dear Kyle,

I hope you don't mind if I call you Kyle, but I believe a request of this nature requires me to be less formal. My name is Roger Powell, and I am a Professor of Archaeology currently working at Entdekung University. I was part of the team re-excavating a site near Saqqara where we have been cataloguing the remains of what we believe to be an ancient Egyptian funeral home. I have come across a most astounding and unusual discovery while X-raying one of the tombs and I was hoping you would be able to shed some light on my findings.
I would like to invite you to visit me at the University of Entdekung in Germany where I would like to show you and to discuss what we have found. I am also hoping that you know someone called Emma and how to get in touch with her.
I know that this is highly irregular, and I am being rather cryptic, but the less I discuss via email the better, although I felt this easier to send than to call you in person.
If I have caught your interest and can persuade you and Emma to visit me here, can you please confirm by replying to my email. Please feel free to check out my credentials which you will find below and to contact me at the university.
We would be more than happy to pay for the expense of yours and Emma's visit.

Yours hopefully,
Roger Powell

Professor of Archaeology Archaeology Department University of Entdekung

The email looks genuine, and I have also checked his credentials here and I have contacted the university. If you agree, I will phone and speak to him at the university.'

Emma sat stunned. 'I don't know what to think. How does he know you? How does he know me?'

'I don't know,' said Kyle.

'Do you think it has anything to do with Amira?' said Emma.

'What else could it be?' said Kyle. 'They discovered a funeral home; perhaps they found her body? We have to go don't you think? I can go without you, but I would rather we went together. Do you want to think about it?' Emma shook her head, and he could see the glint of excitement in her eyes. The next part of their adventure awaited. Their very own mystery which seemed to transcend the test of time.

How could they possibly resist when history was knocking on their door?

Chapter 37 – Emma and Kyle

Emma and Kyle arrived at the University of Entdekung reception as instructed, and before they could even give their name to the receptionist, they saw a man hurrying towards them. In his late fifties with salt and pepper hair, Professor Powell was nearly six feet tall with an athletic build. The professor taught classes three times a week, but he much preferred the outdoors and spent any free time he could doing field work.

Professor Powell turned out to be English. He had been living with his family in Germany since the discovery of the funeral home in 2016. He had a firm handshake and a friendly smile, making both Kyle and Emma feel relaxed.

'I am so glad you were both able to come. Please follow me.' As they followed him through the labyrinth of corridors, he asked them how their journey had been and whether they had settled into the hotel ok. He nodded to people he knew along the way and, eventually, he led them into an empty classroom.

It looked like a school lab with sinks set into benches and stools dotted around with all sorts of scientific apparatus and some impressive electronic devices too.

Towards one end of the room was a small office and to the other, a storeroom. 'We could sit in the office but there isn't much room. This classroom is clear for a few hours so I thought we could sit in here. I also wanted to show you some images, so the projector is useful.

Can I get either of you a drink before we begin? There is a good coffee shop on site so I can ask my assistant.' They had eaten a good breakfast before they had come to the university so agreed they would only have a coffee if the professor wanted one too. After a thought, he nodded his head and took their orders and disappeared into his office to ring his assistant.

'You must be curious as to why I asked you both to come. Or even how I knew to ask you both to come,' the professor said as he came out of his office.

'You could say that Professor,' said Kyle after exchanging a look with Emma.

'Please, call me Roger, and can I call you Kyle and Emma?' At their nod, he smiled and gestured to two stools. 'Please take a seat. I'll just get everything set up and when we have our drinks, I will begin.'

He went to the back of the classroom and turned on the computer to warm it up and then to his office.

Intrigued, Emma and Kyle each sat down; feeling like they were attending a lecture. They grinned at each other. There was a knock on the door and a young man came in; he was probably about 20 years old. He was carrying three coffees and a bag of pastries. 'Professor,' he called.

'Back here,' came the professor's voice from the office. He poked his head out. 'Thanks Sam. Can you put them down out there for me?' Sam smiled at Emma and Kyle, put the coffees and pastry bag on the bench beside them, and at their thanks, waved and left the room.

The professor came back out of the office with a sealed plastic container. Inside were documents, a shard of pottery, small pottery containers, and vases all scaled in plastic bags. He placed the tub on the bench near them and then went to the back of the classroom to open some documents on the computer. Images flashed up on the screen at the front of the classroom.

One of the images was of a mummy, two were of what looked like documents, and the other looked like an X-ray of the mummy. The professor grabbed a stool from the bench in front of them. He passed out the coffees and pastries and then took a seat facing them. They ate their pastries taking in the photos on the screen while the professor collected his thoughts, watching them intently.

'I have gone over this in my mind so many times trying to decide how to begin. So, I'm just going to tell you the facts as I know them just as if I was teaching a class. Show you the evidence and see where it takes us.' He nodded his head, agreeing with himself. 'What I am about to show you and tell you is either some elaborate hoax or a most extraordinary story. I can't decide. But the truth is, if this is a hoax, I have absolutely no idea how it was pulled off.'

He gestured to the images on the screen first. 'We have been X-raying the mummies and cataloguing our findings for a few years as I said in my email.'

'We came across this mummy and, judging by the size, we took it to be a female and, from the positioning within the funeral home, catalogued it as Panya Hadary. The priests were quite meticulous with their paperwork. They made a lot of money and kept their documentation very tidy. Emma sucked in a breath at the name of Panya and glanced at Kyle. She obviously recognised the name but tried to disguise her shock as a cough. She could see that the professor noticed but he made no comment.

He paused for a moment, giving Emma time to comment, but when she didn't enlighten him, he continued. 'When we X-rayed, the mummy expecting to find remains, we found it empty of bones. There were no organs preserved in the jars. The wrappings were padded with … ', the professor paused, rubbing his hand through his hair, 'other scraps of material. There was also salt residue which is used at the beginning of the mummification process. It was as if it was created to resemble a person, but we have no idea to what purpose, which is most extraordinary indeed. From the records, money was paid for the upkeep of the remains and for the preservation of her soul by somebody called Baahir. Only one of the jars contained something. Sealed inside one of the jars we found two letters.'

The professor looked intently at Emma and Kyle. 'This is where you come in.' The professor paused for breath.

'Us?' they asked in unison, looking at each other and back at the professor with confusion.

'How?' said Emma. The professor started to take the items out of the container on the bench. He placed two letters sealed in plastic bags in front of them.

'Before you look at them, let me explain. One of these letters mentions Emma and Kyle. Which led us to you both.'

Seeing their confusion, he continued, wanting to get the whole story out 'We carbon dated both letters. They have been checked and double checked by myself, and I confirm, despite my better judgment, that they are indeed authentic. Both letters date back to 600 bc. What is even more extraordinary, is that they are written in English.'

'You mean you translated them?' asked Kyle, confused.

'No,' said the professor. 'That is what is most extraordinary. They are written in English. There was no translation required and they clearly state Kyle and Emma,' said the professor.

'But how do you know that it was us? There are many Kyles and Emmas out there. Why us?'

'Because' said the professor, at the top of the page there are two illustrations. One is of what looks like a necklace. The other looks remarkably like the emblem at the university you attended, and I now believe work at? One of the students helping on the dig has an interest in emblems. He finds them interesting apparently and asked if we would mind if he researched it looking for historical significance. He matched it to your university. Upon investigating with your university, a professor remembered a paper written by you about an amulet and its possible origins. We have a very good research team, although they don't know the specifics of why the information was requested.'

Emma and Kyle sat there in shock, their hearts pounding. The professor motioned to the letter on the bench. 'Please take a look.' He pointed at a sealed white envelope. I also made copies for you to take with you.' Emma and Kyle smiled their thanks. With shaking hands, they pulled the letters closer to them. They were both handwritten by what looked like the same hand. One was beautifully written as if care had been taken to write it. The other was written hastily as if the writer was in a hurry. They couldn't believe their eyes, for there in front of them was a letter written to them from Amira. Just as the professor had said, there were two sketches on top of the letter. One was a perfect replica of the amulet that both Emma and Kyle recognised at once. The other was a sketch of the emblem of Kyle's university as the professor had said.

To my brave Truth Seeker and my Beautiful Heart.

It seems strange writing to two people that have not yet been born and that I myself will be long gone, just a moment in history, when you are just beginning your stories.

I have so much to thank you for. It is down to your bravery my Truth Seeker and your kindness my Beautiful Heart that I am writing this letter. My children have grown and taken over my husband's shipping business. Abubakar my husband has finally retired, with a little persuasion. I am looking out at my grandchildren arguing over who gets to plant the first seed of the season. It is such a beautiful sight. My husband has found a new hobby. He quite enjoys designing and making jewellery so that keeps him from missing his work.

I have seen so much wonder through your eyes Emma my friend and so much bravery through yours Kyle. I name you now because I feel as though we are true friends that are separated by a little thing called time.

I am content and have a good life. I still help people with my 'Special Dreams' as Mama would say and with my medicinal herbs and potions, but I am ready to hand over to the next generation.

I see more adventure for you both. So do not think that by finding the truth that this is the end of your story. Far from it, I know that it is just the beginning.

I will put this letter in a safe place. Abubakar says he knows just the place. He has a twinkle in his eyes, so I know where he means. Such a secret to have kept for so long. I feel free being able to hand it over to you. I know it will be in safe hands.

We thank you both. May your lives be filled with love and laughter. May Horus protect you both.

Love
Amira (Ami) x

My Darling Abubakar,

I pray this reaches you in time. Tonight is the night my Darling. My Truth Seeker told me so. I have sent our darling Bay to you with this letter. It breaks my heart to put this on him, but I feel that time is of the essence. I have asked him to watch the house, but I fear that he will not get back in time.

I love you my darling and our three beautiful children. You are a good father and husband and I love you with all my heart. You and our children are my world.

I fear my nightmares are about to finally come true and that my brother is going to kill me tonight. Sadly, I still do not know why or how. I believe, somehow, he has drugged me, and I can already feel its effects slowing me down. I fear that my dream is about to come true. It's strange that my gift that has helped so many others deserts me now when I need it most.

Love our babies Abubakar and be the good man that I know you are. Oh, how I miss you already.

Your Amira always xx

The professor watched them intently as they read, trying to take in every facial expression as if he could read their minds. They looked genuinely surprised by the letter's existence, but he could tell that it meant something to them, which was impossible, but he could see it was true. The other letter was from Amira to her husband Abubakar, which Kyle recognised as the letter he asked her to write that day. He could feel tears scratching the back of his throat. He looked at Emma and could see tears running down her face. 'She survived,' she said, reaching for a tissue.

There were so many questions the professor wanted to ask them, but where to start? Emma's phone rang at that exact moment. She apologised and was going to switch it off but after reading the name of the caller said she needed to take it and left the room. The professor decided to wait for her to come back, but when she did, she looked distressed and said they needed to leave. They apologised to the professor and, taking the white envelope, they collected their things and left promising to be in touch soon.

Chapter 38 – Emma and Kyle

Professor Powell watched out of the window of the classroom as Kyle and Emma left the building. He had been curious to meet them and, having met them, he did not think that they could perpetrate a scam of this magnitude. Was the phone call planned to help them leave without explanation? Emma had looked genuinely upset, and from his viewpoint from the classroom, he could see that Kyle was comforting her.

He had purposely left them alone so that he could observe them. From what he could see, they were confused about why he had asked them there. He asked his TA to drop in unannounced to see if he could make out any of their conversation. He then placed his seat facing them so that when he laid out the letter, he could see their reactions.

They were genuinely surprised by the letters; he was sure of that. He even saw tears running down Emma's face, and although they glanced at each other, with what may have been relief, he was not sure; they didn't enlighten him any further on the letters. He could not put aside the fact that the letters, and all the artefacts found with both letters, had been authenticated and the letters carbon dated. He had even checked himself again a couple of days before their visit.

They were either the best actors he had ever met with some serious fraudulent skills, or ..., he couldn't finish the thought. He would not be able to publish his findings. He would be a laughingstock among the archaeological and educational community if he presented such findings. He thought that he would probably never solve this mystery and it didn't sit well with him.

He turned away from the window and packed everything back into the container. He then saved everything onto a disc and deleted all evidence from his computer.

He was the only one who knew the contents of the container and for now it would have to stay that way. He locked the plastic container in his office overnight and would then bury it in the archives tomorrow. The best place for it. Maybe one day in the future it would come to light again and somebody else would be able to solve the mystery.

He didn't sleep well that night, tossing and turning with one bad dream after another. He woke up in the early hours ringing with sweat, the laughter and ridicule of his peers still ringing in his ears. He finally fell asleep again around four only to be rudely awakened by his alarm clock.

He started his journey to work, stopping off to get some coffee and then making his way to his office and classroom. As he entered the building, there was some commotion, and a campus security guard was talking to a police officer. When the security guard spotted the professor, he said something to the police officer and they both turned and walked over to him.

With a sinking feeling he said, 'Hi Joe, is everything ok?'

Joe looked at the police officer and, at his nod, he spoke to the professor. 'I'm sorry Professor Powell but it looks like someone broke into your office last night. We need you to come and have a look sir and see if anything is missing.' Professor Powell followed Joe and the police officer along the corridor to his office. All he could hear was his heart pounding in his ears. He stood in the doorway of his office and looked at the empty space where he had left the container last night. It was a moment before he realised that the police officer had asked him a question.

'Is anything missing professor? Did you have anything valuable in here that someone would want to steal?'

The professor thought fast. He could not tell them about the container, but who would have taken it. Kyle and Emma? He didn't think so. As much as they had looked at the artefacts that accompanied the letters, they weren't valuable enough for them to sell. He had given them a copy of the letters so it seemed unlikely that they would come back for those. Maybe someone didn't want others to see what he had found, what the letters contained. Were Emma and Kyle in danger from being in possession of copies of the letters? Should he tell the police officer to contact them? All this was going around in his head as the police officer put his hand on his shoulder. 'Professor, did you hear me? Is there anything missing? Are you OK sir?'

The professor nodded his head, not sure what question he was answering with that movement. At a nod from the police officer, Joe left and came back with a glass of water, which he passed to the professor. Nodding his thanks to Joe, he slowly sipped, trying to come up with a plausible answer for why someone would break into his office. He couldn't tell them about the container's contents he decided. He hoped he could catch Emma and Kyle before they left Germany. He needed to speak to them, to warn them maybe, he wasn't sure.

Realising the police officer and Joe were both looking at him expectantly, he looked around the room for a lifeline. Spotting his computer on his desk, he nodded. That would be a plausible explanation. 'Professor?' the police officer asked again.

'Sorry, erm, I don't think anything is missing. I won't know until I look more closely but nothing is standing out to me. My computer is still there, but I am just wondering if that might be the reason. It is coming to the end of term and test time. I keep my test papers on my computer.'

The police officer walked over to the computer and moved the mouse. The login screen appeared requesting his password. 'Would anyone be able to access your computer Professor, maybe guess your password?'

Professor Powell tried to look sheepish. 'My password is Cleopatra, it is also my dog's name, although I call her Cleo for short,' embarrassed, he blushed. 'It wouldn't be hard to guess. My students know me well.'

The police officer nodded. 'Maybe it's time to update your password Professor. We will get computer forensics to come and look if that is ok with you. They can also advise you of more secure password options.' The professor nodded. 'They will be in to see you later today. If you aren't available, Joe should be able to show them the way.' Joe walked out of the office to escort the police officer out of the building. The police officer paused in the doorway and, frowning, walked back to the office to examine the door. 'Strange, I can't see any sign of the door being forced. Are you sure you locked the door last night Professor?' Professor Powell nodded his head. He had made sure to lock both his office and classroom door before leaving last night.

When the police officer finally left, the professor remembered the cameras in the hallway. They monitored the corridor from both directions so they would be sure to have picked up whoever had entered his room and stolen the container. He figured that the police officer would already have thought of this but Leon who monitored the security cameras owed him a favour, and this seemed like as good a time as any to call that in.

He waited fifteen minutes to make sure the coast was clear, and that Joe and the police officer had left. He then closed his door and went into his office. He rang Leon on his mobile rather than using the internal phone service, which is what he would normally do. Leon answered on the second ring. 'Prof,' he said. 'Are you OK? I was just going to come and see you.'

'Yes Leon, thank you, a bit shook up.'

Leon did not sound happy. He was ex-military and Professor Powell knew it was part of the military that didn't get spoken about. After retiring early due to injury, he had started his own security firm. He provided security for many prestigious businesses including the university and museums. He took his job very seriously and wouldn't be happy with this breach of his security.

'Did the cameras pick up anything Leon?' asked the professor.

Leon was quiet for a moment and then said, 'You know I can't talk to you about this Prof. The police officer just left. He said you think that it was a student after exam questions, but I'm sensing it is more than that? Am I wrong?' The professor considered Leon to be a good friend and would trust him with his life. Not only did he arrange security for the university, but he would also scope out the safety of locations before Roger and his team began their excavations. They had come up against trouble a few times when local collectors hadn't been happy that they had permission to excavate and remove artefacts from areas that they believed belonged to them.

Excavation sites he had worked on had to be secured sometimes and he had had his hotel room ransacked more than once. He needed to talk to someone about what was going on and he was worried that Emma and Kyle may be in danger knowing what they knew. He didn't know why he thought this, but his gut told him so.

'Can we meet up somewhere Leon? Somewhere private where we can talk?'

Leon gave him directions to a quiet restaurant he knew. 'Let's meet in one hour. Do you need me to monitor your whereabouts Prof?'

'Not sure yet Leon but can you locate two people for me?' He gave Leon Emma and Kyle's details. He was hoping whatever emergency had caused them to leave the university in a hurry hadn't caused them to leave the country too.

'I'm coming over to check your office myself Prof. Why are you in today anyway? I thought it was your day off?'

'It was,' said the professor. 'I needed to put something in archive so I thought I would do it when I had no classes.'

Leon didn't miss anything. 'Was this something in your office by any chance?' The professor's silence spoke volumes. 'Go home Prof, be safe, I will see you later.' The phone went dead, and the professor thought that was a good plan. *Who had broken into his office and took the container and why? Was it to keep it secret? But for what purpose?*

Before Leon went to investigate the professor's office he put in some calls and found that Kyle and Emma were still at the hotel although they were due to leave in a few hours. He sent his most trusted man to speak to them and invite them to the meeting with the professor later. He had already reviewed the security recordings that morning as soon as he knew of the break in. Joe had done the preliminary investigation, but he wanted to retrace the steps he thought that the thief had taken.

One thing he was sure of was that this was a professional who knew what they were doing. What he had seen on the recordings proved this. Not only had they got past his security into the building, which rankled, but they had made off with whatever the professor had locked in his office, and nobody had seen anything. He was not happy at all. He would be conducting a thorough investigation and if any of his men were involved, heads would roll.

Emma and Kyle were packing, ready to leave, when the phone rang. 'It's the front desk,' said Kyle. He picked up the receiver, 'Hello. OK, thank you, we will come down.' At Emma's enquiring look, he advised her that there was someone in reception who Professor Powell had sent.

Standing at the reception desk was a rather imposing man. He was dressed smartly in a suit and when the receptionist indicated Emma and Kyle, he nodded and walked towards them. 'I have come on behalf of Professor Powell,' he said in English, showing them his badge. He was part of a security firm that provided the security at the university. 'He has asked if you would accompany me to meet him at a restaurant near here.'

'We need to go home,' said Kyle.

'A family emergency,' said Emma. 'We were just leaving for the airport.'

He nodded gravely. 'When is your flight?' Their flight was not for a few hours yet, but they wanted to get to the airport to wait. 'I will get you there on time. I promise.'

Kyle and Emma exchanged a worried look. 'Professor Powell would not have asked if it was not urgent. Wait one moment.' He stepped away from them and made a quick phone call speaking in rapid German. Nodding his head, he came back to them. 'I have been given permission to relay some of the facts to you. Early this morning the professor's classroom and office were broken into and the container holding the things he showed you yesterday were taken. They were the only things taken.' He stopped to let them take this in and to observe their reaction, which was obvious shock. 'He was worried about you and wanted to make sure you were ok before you left.'

They both felt as if there was more to the story, but he said no more. 'Do you mind if I just ring the professor?' asked Kyle. The security man nodded and stepped back to give them some privacy.

Kyle took the professor's business card from his wallet and called him on his mobile. He answered in a shaky voice. 'Hello.'

'Professor Powell, it's Kyle.'

'Oh, thank God we managed to catch you. Are you both ok?'

Kyle confirmed they were and felt something starting to roil in the pit of his stomach. 'Shouldn't we be? There is a man here Professor, saying you sent him.'

'Yes, yes, I did. He should be from Schultz security firm. They are the security at the university and his boss is a close friend of mine and one that I trust and have trusted with my life on more occasions than I like to remember. I know you are in a hurry to get home, and this is not good timing at all, but could you please go with him and meet me at the restaurant. Leon is checking the security footage for me, and I want to make sure you know what happened so that you can be cautious. I'm not trying to scare you, but it would be remiss of me not to tell you.'

'OK professor, we will meet you there.'

Kyle filled in Emma quickly trying not to alarm her, but he could see from her face it didn't work. They agreed to go, and after packing their suitcases in the boot, they were whisked off to the restaurant.

The professor was there when they got there and ushered them over to a quiet corner where another man was waiting. He nodded to their escort who stood back and watched the front door. Emma and Kyle took a seat and the professor looked at Emma. 'I hope everything is ok,' referring to her quick departure the day before.

'My father had a suspected heart attack,' said Emma. 'They are doing some tests, but my mom asked if we could come home early.'

'I am so sorry,' said the professor. 'We will get through this as quickly as possible so that you can get to the airport. I do hope your father will be ok.'

'Thank you,' said Emma, and Kyle squeezed her hand gently.

The professor introduced them to Leon who filled them in on the theft.

'I don't want to worry you both, but this was a professional job. Beyond professional. The thief was nothing but a ghost.' He showed both Emma and Kyle the footage on his tablet. There was clearly a figure going down the corridor to Professors Powell's classroom. It entered his office, took the container, and came back out of the professor's office and then disappeared. The figure might as well have been a ghost. It was blurry and had no sustainable shape. You couldn't tell if it was a man or woman. You couldn't tell the height of the person.

'These are top security systems which I created and installed myself and this person left absolutely no trace. Nothing else was taken but the container and its contents. I will be investigating further but I have never in all my years, in my line of work, seen anything quite like this. The professor wanted you both to know as we don't know the purpose of the theft or if you both may be in danger. I have no evidence to suspect this yet, but he wanted you both to be aware.'

'I know this is a lot to drop on you both and you have to leave now but please keep in touch. If there is anything you could tell Leon that would help, please let us know.' said the professor.

Leon handed them his business card. 'If you do for any reason, feel that you are in danger, please call this number. I WILL send help.'

Kyle and Emma felt overwhelmed. Were they in danger? They had no idea who could have taken the items and why they would want to. None of this made any sense. They promised to keep in touch and to let them know if anything else occurred. True to his word, the security guard got them to the airport on time and they were relieved to be going home.

As they sat on the plane absorbing all that they had learnt in the last few days, they felt dazed. They were both amazed by the letter that Amira had written to them. It was astonishing that it had lasted for so long and she had found a way to get it to them. They were overjoyed that she had made it past that horrible night and that she had lived a full and happy life.

Kyle squeezed Emma's hand. 'I love you,' he said.

Emma smiled back at him with tears in her eyes. 'I love you too.'

They went straight to the hospital from the airport so that they could see how Matthew was doing. Chione confirmed that it was a mild heart attack. Her father was going to fully recover but he needed to rest some and make some changes to his lifestyle.

Emma was confident that her mom would make sure that her dad made those changes and went in to see him and gave him a big hug.

Chapter 39 – The Knights of Ramla

Kevin walked into the secret headquarters of The Knights of Ramla carrying the container that he had appropriated from Professor Powell's office. 'Ah good,' said Bay, greeting him. 'Did you get everything?'

Kevin nodded and put the container on the counter. 'I checked the professor's computer, but he had already deleted the files on there. I went in deeper and cleared any residual files so it can't be reinstated. He didn't email anyone that I could see. It seems the professor was unsure what he had found and was reluctant to share it with the educational community at large.'

Bay nodded his thanks. 'I'll take them down to the vault and check them in.' The vault was located under Amira Imports and Exports, which was built later as part of the society's cover. It was the best hiding place and the perfect place to recruit from. 'We should keep an eye on him in case he changes his mind and goes public,' said Bay.

Kevin nodded his head. 'I bugged his computer to flag any mention of what he found. What about Emma and Kyle?' said Kevin.

'We will keep an eye on them,' said Bay.

Kevin nodded, 'Anything else?' Distractedly, Bay shook his head. 'Beer and pool later?' said Kevin.

Bay finally looked at him. 'Sorry my friend,' he said sheepishly. 'Meet at The Rabbit & Hare?' They decided on a time and, nodding, Kevin made his departure.

Bay removed the lid from the container and took out the contents within. With shining eyes, he read the letter written by his ancestor Amira. He loved his job, he thought, placing the letters back in the box. He couldn't wait to tell his father about the letters. Although neither he nor his father had experienced travel themselves, they had both grown up on the stories from a young age. In fact, the amulet was a family heirloom, and the stories were full of important clues and instructions passed down from generation to generation to prepare them for their part in the story. For without them having this knowledge, how could they play their part?

He had been working at The Knights of Ramla for just over 20 years now. He had accomplished so much and was so proud of what The Knights stood for and what they had achieved collectively.

He met Kevin later at The Rabbit & Hare for a couple of drinks and a few racks of pool. Later, they went to the local Italian for a meal. The waiter took their orders and poured them both a glass of wine. 'Cheers!' Clinking glasses, they savoured their first taste of the wine.

'So how is the family? said Bay. Kevin sat very still for a moment. 'Are you ok?' said Bay.

'Wow, déjà vu,' said Kevin, laughing. 'They are good. Izzy is still teaching at the university. The boys have finished university and want to start their own tech company. They dropped this on me last week. They want me to help them set it up.'

'Wow,' said Bay. 'The apples don't fall far from the tree as they say. Impressive. What do you think?'

'It's a good idea. I had to learn everything I know but with them it's almost instinctual. Impressive to see, even for me.' Kevin was one of the best in his field. 'They bought broken PlayStations when they were kids, just to take them apart and see how they worked. They still work now, with some upgrades to them,' Kevin said, smiling. 'We have had lots of fun times playing video games and still get together one Friday a month for beers, pizza, and video games. Just me and the boys. No holds barred.

What about yours? How are Zoe and Sarah?'

'Good. Sarah starts university next month,' said Bay.

'I'm sensing some tension,' said Kevin.

'She wants to do art. Jewellery design in particular. I was worried. I wanted her to do …,' Bay paused, 'something more stable?' Bay smiled sheepishly. 'She sat me down last night for a chat.' Bay was now smiling with pride. 'She is quite a force to be reckoned with my daughter. You should see some of her work. It's beautiful. Arts in her blood she said. When she was little, my dad used to show her Amira's jewellery. She had a few pieces that were designed and made by Abubakar. She said growing up that she wanted to be able to create something that beautiful, but not only that, she also wants to be able to restore art and jewellery and other historical artefacts like her mum. Her own designs she will create for the love of it, but the restoration will be for her love of history. So, she is studying art history, design and technology, and art preservation. She has a vision I didn't expect. I was impressed and felt so proud. She shut me up anyway,' Bay said, smiling.

'I think our children have good futures and, should they want to join, I know the future of The Knights will also be in good hands,' said Bay.

'To our children,' said Kevin, clinking glasses once more.

Chapter 40 – Emma and Kyle

'Do you think we are in danger?' Emma asked. They had arrived back from the hospital a couple of hours ago. Emma's dad was recovering well and joking with the nurses. Emma unpacked while Kyle cooked chicken and pasta for dinner with tomato and basil sauce. They accompanied it with a bottle of wine and were now relaxing on Emma's couch, American football playing quietly on the TV.

The copies of Amira's letters that Professor Powell had given them were laid on the coffee table in front of them. They had read and reread them several times, still unable to believe what they had read.

Giving himself time to gather his thoughts, Kyle went to the adjoining kitchen counter and poured them both a slug of Jack Daniels. He passed Emma a glass and savoured his first swallow as he retook his seat next to her.

'I don't think so,' said Kyle. At Emma's sceptical look, he smiled. 'I mean it.' He gestured to the letters on the coffee table. 'Amira's safe,' he said. 'The letters prove that. Surely that is the end of it. It's not like we could share our story with anyone. I think the information Professor Powell had was a threat to somebody. It was there in black and white. Maybe it was taken to hide it. Or maybe it was destroyed.'

'But what about the letters? We have copies,' said Emma.

'Nobody knows that as far as we know. I can't see Professor Powell saying anything,' said Kyle. 'Besides, the originals have been carbon dated. Ours are just photocopies. Proof of nothing really.'

Emma levelled a steady gaze on Kyle. He held it for a moment and then his gaze strayed away. There was more, she was sure of it. 'This isn't over for you, is it? You want to find out what happened to her that night and after.' Kyle didn't answer straight away. After some thought, Emma got up and went back to the kitchen to fetch the bottle of Jack and brought it back to the couch.

'I want to know too,' Emma said, pouring them both another glass.

'Are you sure?' said Kyle.

Emma nodded. 'Time for some research,' she said, 'starting tomorrow.' She finished her drink and got up off the couch stretching the kinks out of her body. She saw Kyle's eyes follow her movements and stretched again just to see his eyes widen.

She held out her hand towards him in invitation. Kyle downed the rest of his drink feeling it burn down into his belly. He took Emma's hand placing a kiss in the palm. He followed that with a kiss and nibble on her wrist feeling her pulse quicken under his tongue. Emma shivered under the heat of his gaze and the feel of his lips on her wrist.

Kyle pulled gently on Emma's hand, and she sank back onto the couch. He released her hair from its fastening and thread his fingers through its silky waves until it cascaded down her back. He took her mouth in a drugging kiss, parting her lips to mate his tongue with hers.

He kissed a fiery path along her jaw to her ear, which he nibbled gently. At her groan, he kissed down her neck to her shoulder. Unfastening her blouse, he kissed the soft skin above her bra cup, making her shudder with pleasure. He lifted her up so that she straddled his lap on the couch. She looked into his eyes seeing desire had darkened the blue.

He pushed her blouse slowly off letting the silky texture caress her skin before it fell to the floor. Cupping her face gently, he took her mouth in another drugging kiss. He released her mouth, and while she was reviving her lungs with air, he kissed a searing path down her neck. He removed her bra, which joined her blouse on the floor, and gently cupped her breasts.

She loved his large hands. She fit them perfectly, like she was made just for him. She wiggled on his lap feeling the evidence of his desire and he groaned as he took one nipple into the wet heat of his mouth. He swirled his tongue around her nipple, gently massaging her other breast, and her head fell backward as she gasped with pleasure. Kyle sucked gently on her nipple and, needing something to hold onto, she threaded her fingers through his hair clutching his head to her which pushed her breast further towards his mouth, inadvertently deepening the pleasure.

Groaning, he released one nipple and kissed his way across her chest. 'I like to be fair,' he said, looking up at her sexily before taking her other pert and waiting nipple into the hot recess of his mouth, administering the same pleasure until she was squirming on his lap once more. This heightened his pleasure until he released her gasping, 'I think we are definitely wearing too much.'

Chuckling, they started to divest each other of their clothes, kissing and exploring each other as each item of clothing fell to the floor in a messy pile. When they could wait no more, Kyle sank into Emma's heat feeling her tighten around him. They moved together as one before finding their release. Sated, they collapsed into a tangled sweaty heap. They lay there for a few moments catching their breath.

Kyle kissed Emma tenderly on her swollen lips. He stood up, pulling Emma to her feet. Swinging her into his arms and making her squeal, he carried Emma into her room and lay her on the bed. Pulling back the covers, Emma slipped under them. Kyle joined her and she curled happily into his arms. 'I love you,' he said.

'I love you,' said Emma. They shared a gentle kiss, and with Emma's head resting on Kyle's shoulders, they fell asleep.

Chapter 41 – Emma and Kyle

Emma woke up the next morning to the fragrant smell of bacon and freshly brewed coffee. Stretching, she blushed, remembering the night before on the couch. Smiling and humming happily to herself, she put on her dressing gown and walked through to the kitchen.

She found Kyle drinking a cup of coffee at the counter with his laptop in front of him. His hair was still damp from a recent shower, and he was wearing a sky-blue t-shirt and jeans. He looked so sexy she couldn't help but pinch his very cute bottom on the way past into the kitchen. 'Morning,' she said, leaning across the counter to kiss him.

'Morning,' he said, kissing her back. 'Breakfast is nearly ready.' Emma poured herself a cup of freshly brewed coffee and topped his cup up.

Perching on the stool next to him, she glanced at the laptop. 'What are you doing?' she said, looking at the screen.

'I got to thinking this morning. Amira and Abubakar left clues on the letter to help find us. What if there are clues for us too? Breadcrumbs for us to follow. So, I uploaded a photo of Amira's amulet that Abubakar illustrated on the letter. It's currently searching to see if there are any matches.'

Emma could see that the computer had a way to go before it finished its search. 'While I dish up, why don't you make a list of anything you can remember from speaking to Amira over the years. Any names of people or places. Any pictures that you drew. Anything that could help with our research.' Emma got a notepad and pen and sat down at the kitchen table. Kyle put a glass of orange juice in front of her and a plate of toast in the middle of the table and then went back to the kitchen. Emma tried to rack her brain for any details that could be useful in their search. Frustratingly, she was coming up blank.

Kyle dished up bacon, sausages, eggs, and beans which he put in front of her. He also placed brown sauce and ketchup in front of her. 'In case you want to destroy it,' he said, winking. He then sat down with his plate.

'Thank you. It looks and smells delicious.' He noticed her empty notepad.

'Maybe I'm trying too hard?'

'It can wait. Dig in,' he said, and they started on their breakfast.

'Maybe I could talk to mom,' said Emma. 'She might have pictures and stories that I wrote when I was little and used to play with Amira.'

'That sounds like a good idea,' said Kyle.

'I will call her later.'

'OK, what else do we know?' said Kyle.

'We could try and track down the owner of the amulet. I could contact them through the museum,' said Emma.

'Good idea,' said Kyle. 'I could write to my old school too. I know it has been a long time, but they might still have records of Professor O'Hare. He must be connected somehow.'

After they finished their breakfast, Emma called her mom and Kyle sent an email to his old school. Emma finished the call with her mom. 'Mom has boxes of my pictures in the attic. She said I could go over tomorrow and have a look and she would cook me Sunday roast. I wish you were staying longer; I feel like we are so close to something.' Kyle did too and walked over to give Emma a kiss and a hug. He was due to fly home tomorrow. He had lectures next week, otherwise he would have tried to extend his visit.

He was near the end of the term, and he was planning to come back for the six weeks holiday. 'I'll be back before you know it,' he said gently. The truth was he didn't want to go. He felt like he was home and every time he had to say goodbye at the airport and fly home it broke his heart a little.

'Why don't I get a taxi to the airport instead of you dropping me off,' said Kyle, but Emma was already shaking her head. She knew he was trying to spare her a teary goodbye at the airport, but she wanted to spend every second she could with him.

'Maybe when you visit next time, we could discuss plans. I'm sure I could find work in England, or you could here,' said Emma. Already she wanted to cry. Her apartment already felt empty, and he hadn't even left yet.

She didn't want to be without him even for a day. She wanted to weave him into her daily life. She wanted to go to sleep in his arms and wake up to his sleepy smile in the morning. Kyle squeezed her tight, sensing how she was feeling.

They were pulled out of the moment by a *bing* coming from the computer. 'The search must have finished,' said Kyle. He kissed the top of Emma's head, and after another squeeze, he reluctantly released her. Holding her hand, he walked over to the computer.

It had indeed finished its search and had flagged up some matches which fitted the emblem of Amira's amulet. A couple of articles were about the amulet itself and talked of the presentation of it to various museums, one of which was the museum where Chione and now Emma worked. Kyle felt a little frustrated that nothing else had been flagged.

He gave Emma a hug and a kiss. 'Let's get dressed and go out and have some fun.'

Finally, after a week back in England, he got an email from his old school. They couldn't pass on details to him, but Professor O'Hare had agreed that he was happy for them to send an email to them from Kyle.

Kyle composed an email and sent it off. He sat back from the computer feeling excited at following another line of enquiry.

At the headquarters of The Knights of Ramla, Christopher burst into Bay's office unannounced. Thankfully, he was alone. He looked up from his computer, his eyebrow raised at Christopher's entrance as the door bounced off the wall with the force of his entry.

'Sorry,' Christopher said sheepishly, 'but you are not going to believe who contacted me.' He passed the email from Kyle to Bay.

He waited for Bay to read the email. 'What should I tell him?'

Bay thought for a moment. 'Arrange entrance for him to the library.'

'To your family archive?' said Christopher. Kyle was privileged indeed as not many people had been allowed access to the Isson family archive.

Chapter 42 – Kyle

Something was going on in the outer library. Kyle and Mick were deep in the archives, and they could hear it. Mick looked at Kyle and then the armed guards at the door. Even they looked nervous, which wasn't a good sign at all.

They had received special permission from the ancestors of Amira and Abubaker Isson to visit the archives at the Egyptian National Library. It was a one-time only kind of deal that their benefactor had called in a debt to allow them access to. They had struck gold as far as information available, but this would take time to catalogue. They wouldn't have the chance to return, and they certainly weren't going to let them take it with them.

The shouts were getting louder as well as the bangs, which they could only assume was gunfire. This couldn't be good. Mercenaries set on destroying everything around them? The library had had a bout of attempted thefts in the last couple of months and had increased security. They were amazed they could hear anything at all, they were so far down in the depths of the building.

Not many people knew of the archives. Only people with the right connections and with some serious cash. They considered themselves privileged to be allowed access. The two men sent to watch them were none too pleased having them there.

When Kyle and Mick had arrived at the library, a very wary librarian had led them down many flights of steps through many corridors and locked doors, each one darker and dustier that the other. They could only imagine that they didn't have many visitors. Kyle's mind whirled at the thought of what lost and hidden treasure they held within these walls. The archives they were being allowed access to were from a private collector. Kyle wondered if the artefacts were even documented outside of these walls and if anyone in the academic sector even knew they existed. Questions he would never get answers to, he was sure.

He was pretty sure that their unwilling escort took them through the same corridors more than once to disorient them. He needn't have bothered. Kyle was sticking to him like glue. He had no intention of being lost down here. He could only imagine that he didn't want them to return and rob the place. Lost in his thoughts, Kyle looked up to find he was no longer in front of him. With his heart in his throat, he looked behind him, relieved to see that Mick and one of the guards were still here.

The little man leading them suddenly reappeared from around one corner realising they were no longer with him. He nodded his head at Kyle once and turned around and carried on. They all followed closely. 'We should have brought breadcrumbs,' said Mick directly behind him. Kyle chuckled and nodded his head.

Their escort was a small twitchy man. He finally stopped in front of a door and selected two ornate keys from the many pockets of his coat. Apparently, he didn't like cumbersome key rings. He led them into the room, which was surprisingly modern inside, and well-ventilated and carefully lit so as not to harm its contents. Giant filing cabinets, shelves, and storage units of all descriptions filled the perimeter of the room.

There were a few tables and chairs in the middle of the room. Fabric gloves were given to them to protect the artefacts and papers from being damaged.

Glass cabinets held relics of all descriptions, including amulets and other jewellery. Kyle and Mick would have loved a closer look, but their time was limited, and they only had permission to access the information required for their research. Their guide looked fidgety, like he wanted them to leave as soon as they could.

'Watch them,' he said to the guards as he left. 'I'll be back in two hours precisely,' was his parting shot in their direction. They didn't waste any time getting stuck in. They knew how precious their time was. Kyle and Emma had pieced together a family tree for both Amira and Abubaker. They had their parents' names and where they lived when they met. Kyle and Mick were hoping to confirm this in the archives and try and find out what happened to Abubakar, Amira, and their three children. They believed that Amira had been killed by her brother and could be found local to Tara where she grew up.

They couldn't imagine that Abubakar and the children would have wanted to stay around the area after she went missing. They had found lists of births, deaths, and marriages before. There were also laws around selling and importing so they were confident that they would be able to locate Abubakar on this as he had the makings of a fine businessman and they believed that he had grown his father's business. They also felt that Abubakar would have sought shelter with his friends Tifi and Saju.

Kyle was startled from his musings by more shouts and commotion. Whoever was causing all the disturbance was getting louder and possibly closer. The guards exchanged looks and Kyle knew their time was going to be cut a lot shorter than they required. Kyle felt frustration build within him. They wouldn't get another chance, which had been made clear to them. They needed more time; it was too important for their research. This was personal.

He looked over at Mick who was looking furtively towards the door. With a sinking feeling, Kyle tried to catch his eye and subtly shake his head to dissuade Mick from doing what he obviously intended. Mick was stubbornly ignoring him, and Kyle was frantically trying to come up with another plan, but it was too late. Mick grabbed a stack of files from the table in front of him, and taking advantage of the guards' distraction, he ran for the door and down the hall.

Mick moved impressively fast. At five foot five, he was a stocky man and resembled a bulldog. He had a quick sense of humour, was a loyal friend, and a man you wanted on your side when you were backed into a corner. His intelligence was off the scale, and although Kyle was doubtful, he would be able to make it out of the building without help, he was confident that Mick would have memorised every twist and turn. He was also extremely stubborn, and Kyle wondered what was going through his thick skull to think he could get away with his escape.

The guards went running after him, and then one guard thought better of it. He turned around and Kyle tried to look innocent as he glared at him accusingly. He then promptly locked him in the room and ran off in pursuit of Mick. Mick was obviously trying to buy time. Not wanting to waste any, Kyle quickly sifted through the papers looking for specific details. He removed his phone from its hiding place. They had been told to leave them behind or have them confiscated.

With this in mind, they had both fashioned hiding places within their clothing. He took photos of all the pertinent paperwork. He would have liked to have taken some like Mick, but he knew the guards would be more suspicious now and he wasn't leaving here without them thoroughly searching him.

It wasn't long before he heard someone coming down the corridor towards the door. He quickly tidied up the paperwork. He didn't want them knowing exactly what he had been looking for. He turned towards the door as he heard metal scraping against the lock and braced himself for the entrance of a very unhappy and possibly angry guard.

The door opened slowly, and if he had thought he could make it out of the building without help, he would have made a break for it. He squared his shoulders, as prepared as he could be. Then Mick poked his head around the door and winked at him. Smiling, he shook his head at him. 'Come on,' said Mick. Kyle followed him out into the deceptively quiet corridor. Looking both ways, he nodded in one direction. 'Did you get what you needed?' At the nod of Kyle's head, he started running down the corridor with Kyle hot on his heels.

'Do you know where you are going?' Mick just laughed and Kyle realised the rogue was actually enjoying himself. He couldn't help but laugh too as the adrenaline coursed through his body. Mick led him down a labyrinth of corridors left and right and Kyle was concerned they were lost when Mick stopped at a door. Putting his shoulder to it, he forced it open into a quiet alleyway. Kyle shielded his eyes against the glare of the sun, trying to get his bearings.

Mick indicated to him to go back inside the corridor and hold the door partially closed. Kyle reluctantly went back into the corridor looking left and right to make sure it was still empty. Mick ran down the alleyway and disappeared around the corner. Heart pounding in his ears and sweat trickling down his back under his shirt, Kyle waited, straining to hear in the darkness of the corridor. *No footsteps*, he thought with relief, *maybe a few rats, but he would settle for that.*

He heard Mick call his name quietly outside the door and, relieved, stepped back out into the sunlight. They ran back down the alley and bundled into the waiting cab. Mick gave directions and they sat back for the ride. 'That's not our hotel,' he whispered to Mick. Mick winked and shook his head not willing to discuss anything in earshot of the cab driver.

They arrived at a motel and Mick paid the cab driver. He walked past the reception without stopping and led the way up the staircase. Kyle followed, not speaking. Mick stopped at a door, took out a key, and let them into the room. When Kyle entered, he realised that Mick had had all their belongings moved from the hotel they were staying in, and they were waiting in the room.

Kyle turned to a grinning Mick and lifted his eyebrow. 'You've been busy.' Still grinning from ear-to-ear, Mick went to his backpack and pulled out a bottle of Jack. He got two glasses and poured them both a healthy slug. Kyle gratefully took the glass and sank onto one of the wooden chairs beside a very rickety table. Now the adrenalin had left his system, he felt shaky. Kyle took a good mouthful of the whiskey feeling it burn down his throat to his belly. He then took another gulp feeling himself calm down.

Mick watched him for a moment and then nodded his head, confident the whiskey had done its work. 'Always have a back-up plan,' he said cryptically with a wink.

'I think it's time to go home while we still can,' said Kyle.

Mick nodded his head. 'I'll make some phone calls,' he said.

While waiting for one of his contacts to come through for them, they filled up on takeout that Mick ordered and swilled it down with beer. Mick was definitely someone you wanted on your side in a fix.

True to form, his phone rang, and Mick had secured them a flight in the early hours of the morning. There was only an hour to wait before a car would collect them to take them to a private airstrip. Neither felt they could sleep so they looked over the information they had gleaned from the library archives.

Kyle knew he wouldn't be able to rest easy until they had left and were safely on home soil once more. They gathered their things together and paid at the desk as they left the back street motel. They bundled everything into the car waiting for them and Kyle held his breath as they made their way through the quiet streets. Every turn they took he expected to hear sirens or come up against a roadblock to stop them leaving.

He didn't breathe an easy breath until the plane took off and they were on their way home. He texted Emma to say he was on the way home and that he would ring her later to tell her what they had found. He closed his eyes as tiredness finally overtook him.

Chapter 43 – Kyle

Kyle couldn't wait to ring Emma and fill her in on what they had found in the library, but jetlag took over and he slept well into the afternoon and through two missed calls from Emma as well as a few texts.

He quickly texted her that jetlag had knocked him out. He would have a shower and get something to eat and call her when his brain was functioning again.

When he called her, she answered on the first ring, making him chuckle at her eagerness.

He apologised for keeping her hanging and filled her in on their adventure, making her gasp out loud. 'You could have gotten into serious trouble,' she said. After a pause she followed it up with, 'You have all the fun.' Making him laugh out loud.

'I don't know who the private owner was Em, but you should have seen this place. I could have spent years in there cataloguing and still have more to do. It was a veritable treasure trove. I felt like a kid in a candy shop.'

'I'm so jealous,' said Emma. 'So, did you find any treasure?' she said, holding her breath.

'Yes,' said Kyle, pausing to get a reaction. Emma made a noise that he could only describe as a growl.

'OK, OK,' he said.

'We came up with three bits of really important information.

I think we can figure out where Tara is, the village where Amira grew up.'

'Really?' Emma gasped.

'Yes sweetheart.' Kyle said, knowing what that would mean to Emma.

'I was wondering about getting in touch with Professor Powell and seeing if he would be interested in an expedition. We could pool resources from our universities and maybe the museum. What do you think?'

'I think he would be interested. We did kind of leave him hanging,' said Emma. 'He did take the trouble to seek us out.'

'OK,' said Kyle. 'I will give him a call.'

'What else did you find?' asked Emma.

'We found a family tree,' said Kyle. 'I think it is Amira and Abubakar's. I would love to know who owns that collection. We also found some reference to The Knights of Ramla. It kept popping up in various texts that I came across. Does the name sound familiar to you?' said Kyle.

'No,' said Emma. 'Wait,' she said after some thought. 'Amira's neighbour was called Ramla. I can't believe I forgot that. She nursed Amira's brother when he was hurt. It can't be a coincidence can it?'

'Could be, but my gut is telling me it's connected. One of my mate's brothers is a conspiracy nut. He loves researching about secret societies and illuminati and is connected to lots of chat rooms about it. I'll ask him to do some digging and see what he comes up with.

I'll send you all the photo's I've taken, and you can cross-reference the names with ones you wrote as a child.

Once we have a chance to study them, we can exchange info.'

'How is the packing going?' said Emma.

Kyle looked around his chaotic apartment. 'Slowly,' he said laughing. 'I didn't realise how much stuff I had.'

The lease was up on his apartment in a month, and he was moving in with Emma.

They were both beyond excited at the prospect of starting their next chapter together. He was going to be heading up a research project for the university and teaching part-time on secondment at the university in America where Emma worked part-time alongside the museum.

'You sure you can fit me in?' said Kyle, only half joking.

All his furniture had homes to go to and he was only taking personal items but that was turning out to be more than he thought.

'I can't wait,' said Emma.

They said their goodbyes and Kyle looked around. He had another couple of weeks at work to prepare the kids for the end of year. He had better get stuck in as he still had lots to do. He could feel the excitement of adventure sing in his blood with the adventure of Amira taking a backseat for a moment.

Remembering his conversation with Emma, he called his friend to see if his brother could investigate The Knights of Ramla. His friend said he would ask him and pass on Kyle's details so that he could contact him if he found anything.

He then sent an email to Professor Powell filling him in on his visit to the library and what he had found and asked him if he would be interested in pooling resources to excavate the location where he believed Amira had grown up.

Chapter 44 – Kyle

His class were restless this morning. Tomorrow, they left for their first dig, and they were eager to put their theories to the test and get their hands dirty. It was also Kyle's last day before he moved to America and a couple of months before he started his secondment.

Kyle stepped away from the whiteboard, put his pen down, and sat on the front of his desk facing the class, just as Andrew piped up with 'Do you remember your first-time sir?'

This was received by chuckles across the classroom and Kyle raised his eyebrows at Andrew who was now as red as his hair.

Andrew was a smart lad but sometimes he forgot to engage his brain before he opened his mouth. As the laughter died down, Andrew mustered his courage and reworded his question. 'I meant; do you remember your first dig sir?'

'Yeah, for all of us excavation virgins out here.' This was shouted from the back of the class. This time when the class laughed, Andrew laughed too.

Kyle smiled back and waited for the laughter to stop before he answered. 'I remember it like yesterday.' He pointed to the double doors at the back of the classroom which led outside.

'Why don't we have the rest of the lesson outside, and I will tell anyone who wants to listen?'

This was met with whoops, chairs scraping back, and chattering voices as they gathered their things to head outside.

Smiling to himself, Kyle grabbed his things too. As he went to put his phone in his pocket, it buzzed with a message.

He looked up and his students were still on their way out, so he checked it quickly. It was from his friend's brother who he had asked to research The Knights of Ramla for him.

He quickly opened the message. *Are you free later?* it read. *I have info.* Kyle sent a message to meet him later at his and said he would throw in a pizza. He received a thumbs up in return. He put his phone in his pocket and followed the students outside.

As they settled down, he thought back to his first dig. Like he had told his students, he really did remember it like it was yesterday.

'I remember crawling around in the sand and rocks, the unbearable heat of the sun. Trying to cover every part of my body to prevent myself being burnt to a crisp. I also remember the excitement and anticipation of what we might find. It is painstaking, backbreaking work, chiselling away at rock and gently brushing away sand from possible pieces of history just below your feet. We collected the sand into small baskets by hand to move it from one spot to another. There was always the chance of flooding or a sandstorm putting back what had taken us hours to remove.

Some of the men found deep shafts leading from above ground into the earth and believed that if they could make it down the shaft to a tunnel below, they could potentially work their way back to the area we were excavating and find what we were looking for from below. This was dangerous work and not for the faint hearted. It's not like we had a long extendable ladder or climbing gear. A blacksmith was called out from the local town and ladders were attached one by one to the wall and to each other, with drops in between each ladder, in an effort to make it down as far as they needed to go.

I remember one morning I was uncovering a very interesting piece of rock. It no longer resembled just a lump of rock because I could see features beginning to appear beneath the sand. With excitement building, I painstakingly removed dirt and debris from around what was slowly appearing to be a head about the width of my hand. I had uncovered a nose and partial cheek, and as I gently brushed away dirt, I heard a cry from one of the shafts. Jumping into action with others around me, I ran to the supplies to get some ropes. As we got to the mouth of the shaft, we could see that one of the ladders had come away from the wall and a man was dangling precariously with nothing but blackness beneath him. We lowered the rope to him and pulled him to safety. He was a bit grazed and shaking but thankfully had no other injuries.

Do you want to hear the crazy part? Not a half hour later he was being lowered back into the hole with rope and tools to reattach the ladder. They pulled him back up and then lowered him again with rope, tools, and another ladder, which he attached further down. They did this over and over creating a very frightening and precarious climb into the depths below.

What is it about history that enthrals us so …? The thought of discovering something that has not been discovered before? All I know is, that pull is so strong that we are willing to risk our lives, and others' it would seem. I know the feeling that grips me when I start to uncover something from the ground that has been lying hidden for far, far longer than I have been on the planet. Once this feeling has you in its grip, it is very difficult to extricate yourself from its clutches, and when you are back home sitting in your kitchen eating your breakfast going about a normal day, it's as if history calls to you from the sand. Like a lost lover waiting for your next embrace. That is very seductive indeed.

The excavation took time and working down into the shafts was dangerous work. Once they finally made it down to the bottom of the shaft and the tunnel beneath, they found it was prone to flooding and infested with snakes and rats, making it a very unpalatable task and not for the fainthearted or squeamish. We were very lucky that nobody was hurt in the process. This was not always the case, and when someone was hurt, it was a very sobering wake-up call to the perils that we faced in our quest to seek the truth of what was hidden beneath and away in history...'

Kyle came back to the present and looked up sheepishly, expecting to find all his students had disappeared, but he looked up into the faces of every student in his class. They had all stopped to listen, and not only that, they were all giving him their full attention. He didn't even get that in his lessons even though he knew his students enjoyed his classes, as his reviews proved.

'Class dismissed!' he shouted. 'Get some rest everyone, you are going to need it. It's going to be an adventure.' There were murmurs of, 'Thank you sir. We wish you were coming with us sir,' but nobody moved. He looked around but none of his students would meet his eyes.

He then heard a rustle behind him and turned to find Melanie, one of his star students, smiling at him as she held out a gift bag. 'We wanted to give you this to say thank you for being such a great teacher.'

Surprised and touched, he took the bag and looked inside and laughed out loud. He looked up to see that all of his students were looking at him and smiling now. Out of the bag he took an Indiana Jones-style hat which he put on his head to the cheer of his students, and of course, this wouldn't be complete without the Indian Jones whip. He stood up and struck a pose. 'What do you think?' Laughing, his students cheered.

'Thanks everyone. Enjoy your excavation. You are all going to be great, and I am going to miss you all.'

He had made the final arrangements that week for his belongings and he couldn't wait to settle in with Emma.

Chapter 45 – Kyle

At the knock, Kyle opened the door to Will and stopped dead.

Laughing, Will did a little turn on the spot. 'Not what you expected?'

Kyle stepped aside to let him in.

'I grew out of the geeky stage a good few years ago. I'm studying at university now. I want to specialise in art history and symbology and intend to teach.

My mum convinced me that if I wanted a serious career or to be taken seriously for that matter it was time to get rid of the beach bum look. Her words not mine.' Will grinned at him, showing off his straight white teeth.

'Turns out the ladies really like a man in a suit too. I guess I have my mum to thank for that also. Don't tell her I said that though. Why didn't anyone tell me before?'

It was true; if he hadn't been expecting Will, Kyle didn't think he would have recognised him. Gone was the long hair, flashy t-shirts, and sloping shouldered stance.

Will now had a sharp haircut, a slim blue suit, and stood with confidence and pride.

'I can't wait to tell you what I found,' said Will, sounding just like an excited boy. 'I might have changed on the outside but that doesn't mean I've lost the inner geek.' He laughed.

Kyle slapped him on the back. 'Come on through. Pizza is on the way. Let me grab some beers and you can do your presentation professor. I'm sorry about the mess but I'm moving next week.'

'You joke,' said Will, 'but there will be slides.' He held up his laptop and wiggled his eyebrows.

Will set up his laptop on the coffee table. He had even brought a projector with him, and Kyle cleared a space so that he had a clear wall to project onto.

When they were settled down with a couple of beers, Will began. 'From what I can find out, The Knights of Ramla have been around a long time. There are some really old family names coming up connected to this and it has been passed down through bloodlines like a rite of passage.

In more recent years, it looks like they have recruited from outside too. I guess as technology changes, they must adapt to survive.

Based on what you sent me, I also found Amira Imports and Exports. Again, this has been around since Egyptian times, although the name has altered. It consisted of a few cargo ships then and now has grown into ships, lorries, trains, and airplanes. It is something to behold.

They are based at Canary Wharf in London, and I think that this is where you will find the Knights too.'

'Doesn't sound very secret if it was that easy to work out,' said Kyle.

'Well, I don't want to blow my own trumpet,' said Will, 'but I had to do some serious digging to find what I did, and I called in a few favours. I've probably made it sound simpler than it was.

The emblem and the names you gave me link them together. I'm not sure everyone would have that knowledge. How did you come by them, by the way?' said Will, looking at Kyle intently.

'That's a long story. You finish first and I will fill you in,' said Kyle, feeling that he could trust Will.

'OK. So, to what they do,' said Will. 'The main reason they formed was as a protection. Now this is the bit you might find hard to believe.' Will paused and looked at Kyle. He assessed him for a minute. 'Or maybe you won't,' he said, raising his eyebrows.

'OK, I'm just going to come out with it. I think they were formed to protect time travellers. To enable them to complete their missions.' He waited to see how Kyle responded.

'Missions?' was all he said.

'Yes. There are all sorts of stories about time travellers, most of which have been ridiculed. None of them were frivolous, and they seem to have meaning of some kind. Like, saving a life, or lives.

There are some really influential people who are part of this. Old family names and serious money. I think their base is designed to send a message too. If anyone figured out about The Knights their base says "We Are Powerful. Do you know what you are taking on?"

'You sound like you want to join,' joked Kyle.

'Hell yes,' said Will. 'That would be a dream come true. Imagine their resources. The information they must have access to.'

Thinking of the library, Kyle had to agree.

'I figure the more knowledge I gain and the more obscure my talents, I might catch their interest,' said Will. 'Who knows?'

Yes, indeed, thought Kyle, who knows?

'So, are you going to tell me what this is all about?' said Will.

'I'll tell you over pizza,' said Kyle, heading for the door as the bell rang. So, Kyle told Will about his experiences of meeting Amira, about the amulet, and about the library.

When he had finished, Will let out a low whistle. 'Wow man!' was all he managed.

All of the puzzle pieces were finally coming together.

When Will left, Kyle called Emma and filled her in on Will's findings. 'I think we should go,' he said.

'What, just turn up on their doorstep?' said Emma.

'Why not?' said Kyle. 'What do we have to lose? They know about us. In fact, I think they have played a big part in all of this. Plus, I think we have a way in. Professor Christopher O'Hare. He brought the amulet to me all those years ago. It must have been him that got me an invitation to the library. He must be part of The Knights. I say we walk through the door and ask to speak to him.' Kyle paused to draw breath.

He heard Emma puff out a breath on the other end of the phone. 'I'm in,' she said.

Chapter 46 – Emma and Kyle

It would be some time before they went to Canary Wharf. With Kyle moving in with Emma and starting his secondment, and then Professor Powell contacting him to say he was interested in joining their group in their quest to find Tara, the months flew by.

Between Emma, Kyle, and Professor Powell they managed to get the funding required for their excavation and made their plans to travel to Egypt.

It was getting dark by the time they made camp at the coordinates they believed to be Tara where Amira grew up. They were tired, hot, and dusty, but they were excited at the same time.

Their team consisted of Kyle, Emma, Professor Powell, and Mick as well as two of Kyle's students, a colleague of Emma, and two colleagues of Professor Powell. They each brought their own specialisms, and they were all passionate about the excavation.

The next morning Kyle woke up first and walked around the site to stretch his legs. Looking around him, he stopped in his tracks. He made his way quickly back to their tent and found Emma getting dressed. She looked at Kyle expectantly as he burst into the tent, and he just smiled at her.

She quickly finished dressing and, taking her hand, Kyle led her out of the tent and stopped in the spot he was in a moment ago.

He pointed at the pyramid in the distance. 'This is it,' he said excitedly. 'This is where I first met Amira. She was standing just over there; obviously, a lot has changed, but that,' he said, pointing to the pyramid again, 'that I remember. It was still being built then.'

Chapter 47 – Emma, Kyle, and The Knights

Christopher was just going over his itinerary for the week when his desk phone rang. It was Ann on reception, so he picked it up with a cheery hello.

'Hello Christopher, I have a couple in reception asking for you,' said Ann.

'Oh,' said Christopher, 'I don't have any appointments until later.'

'They said their names are Emma and Kyle. They said if I mentioned their names and amulet you would want to speak to them. They look really nervous. Do you want me to call security?'

'No, that's ok Ann, I know them. I forgot they were coming that's all,' he improvised. 'I'll be down in ten.'

A smile spread across Christopher's face. He was impressed they had tracked him down. He quickly made his way to Bay's office and knocked on the door.

Bay called out for him to come in and he entered quickly. Noting Bay was alone, he hurriedly closed the door.

'Guess who is here? You'll never guess. Emma and Kyle,' he said not giving Bay a chance to answer.

'Are you ready to meet them?' said Christopher.

Bay nodded. 'I think it is time, don't you?'

Chapter 48 – Emma and Kyle

It was so nice meeting Bay. So many pieces of the puzzle began to fit into place. How the amulet came to be at Kyle's school, the benefactor that arranged his scholarship. Bay and The Knights were clearly behind his admission to the library. The only question this didn't answer was why them? Why did the amulet choose them?

Bay assured them he also had the answer to this question and invited them to his home in Surrey to explain further.

Arrangements were made and a few weeks later Kyle and Emma were approaching Bay's home along a tree-lined lane. The trees were tall and thick with green foliage creating a leafy tunnel allowing dapples of sunlight through at intervals.

The lane led to a gravel driveway which opened up into the front of the house.

They were both blown away by the sheer size of the house. It was built of red and brown brick with white Georgian windows. Kyle drove around the central island of lawn and parked the car.

They walked up the four steps to the large wooden door set in an arched frame, surrounded by an arch of sandstone brick with a coat of arms at the apex of the archway.

Holding hands, they rang the bell. They turned around to admire the view while they waited for someone to answer the door.

'Do you think they have servants?' Emma whispered to Kyle. Kyle squeezed Emma's hand, hearing the nerves that made her voice quiver.

They turned around as they heard the door being opened. It was opened not by some severe butler but by Bay himself, who greeted them with a friendly smile.

He was a handsome man in his mid-fifties, with an athletic build. He had jet black hair which was going grey slightly at the temples and his eyes crinkled at the edges and sparkled with kindness when he smiled.

'Welcome,' he said, greeting Emma with a kiss on the cheek and Kyle with a hearty handshake. 'Come in, come in,' he said, stepping back and gesturing for them to enter.

'Your home is beautiful,' said Emma as she stepped inside.

'Thank you,' said Bay. 'It has belonged in our family for generations.'

The front door led straight into an open-plan living room which reached up two stories. There was natural wooden flooring throughout which was two shades lighter than the wooden panelling on the walls. A large fireplace was set in one wall. The upper part of the room was painted white as was the ceiling, which had intricate pattens set into it and around the edges. The coving was also in wood with intricately carved detail.

Light filtered through the open doorway into the room as well as from three large Georgian windows, one of which was above the doorway, one to the right of the doorway on the lower level, and the other above the window on the upper level.

In front of the fire was a large rug of red and pale blue in a Georgian-style design with a highly polished oval coffee table in the centre. This was surrounded by a red sofa and two chairs. Everywhere the eye could see there was antique furniture as well as vases and ornaments.

Emma took in the rest of the room. All the antique furniture was highly polished, expensive, and truly beautiful.

'Let's go through to the library first,' said Bay. 'There is something I want to show you.'

He led them down a long hallway through a doorway to the right. The library was bigger than Kyle and Emma's living room and kitchen put together. Again, it was decorated with various antiques. The wall to their left had two floor-to-ceiling Georgian windows with green and gold-patterned curtains. The wall was painted an olive green.

The wall ahead of them had two floor-to-ceiling bookcases packed with books. The surrounding wall was painted a forest green. The floor had the same wood panelling as the living room.

Again, a large Georgian rug sat in the centre of the room. This one in red, blue, and green. It had three leather chairs the same shade of forest green as the back wall. In the centre of the rug was a wooden table with a green leather top, which also matched the chairs.

Their taste was exquisite, and Emma couldn't keep her eyes from darting around the room at all the beautiful furniture. She wondered what treasures the rest of the property held.

On the right-hand side was a large mahogany desk with a matching green leather top and leather chair behind it.

'Please have a seat,' said Bay. 'Can I get you a drink? I have tea, coffee, or something stronger if you would prefer.'

They settled on drinks and took some time to get reacquainted. He asked about their journey, and they asked about his family.

Inevitably, the conversation came around to Amira. 'The story goes,' said Bay, 'that after that night, Abubakar hired a nanny and took the children to start over.

They stayed with their friends Tifi and Saju and then moved on to make a new home. The nanny loved the children like her own and Abubakar and she fell in love and married.'

'But Amira didn't die,' said Emma. 'We have Amira's letter.'

Smiling, Bay nodded his head. 'Amira and the nanny are one and the same,' said Bay. 'Abubakar didn't want Amira to be in danger to Baahir ever again, so they crafted a new story.'

'Did they ever see him again?' said Kyle.

'Not that I know of,' said Bay. 'Abubakar kept tabs on him for a while, but the trail went cold. I think Abubakar decided he was no longer a threat and wanted to get on with their lives.

Abubakar was a fine artist,' said Bay. 'Would you like to see some of his drawings?'

'I would love that,' said Emma.

Bay went to his desk and gently picked up a portfolio and handed it to Emma.

She gasped as she opened the portfolio to the drawings kept safely within. They were in plastic wallets to protect them.

They were exquisite. There was a series of drawings depicting Amira as a young girl into older age. Not stiff drawings but action drawings of Amira laughing, working in her garden with her hair slightly covering her face from the sun as she worked. Amira smiling with such love she could only be looking at Abubakar. Amira holding babies and then toddlers. There were drawings of their children at various stages of growth.

There were pictures of the amulet that he had designed and had made to give to Amira when he proposed, as well as other jewellery he had designed. 'These are beautiful,' said Emma. 'All of them.' She could feel the joy coming from the subjects of each picture.

Smiling, Bay pointed at some of the drawings of jewellery. 'He made some of those. We have them in the safe. I could show you later if you would both do me the honour of staying for dinner.'

Emma nodded and looked over at Kyle, but he was occupied by some miniatures in a glass cabinet she had spotted when they first came in. 'Kyle?'

He turned around at the sound of his name, a strange smile on his face. He looked at Emma. 'We would like that. Thank you.'

'I have one final question.' said Emma. Bay merely smiled. 'Ok, maybe not my last,' she said laughing. At Bay's nod she asked, 'Why us?'

Bay didn't need to ask what she meant. He looked at Kyle and then Emma. 'I believe the amulet chose Kyle. It knew you were destined to be together and needed to right a wrong to make sure that happened.'

'How do you mean?' said Emma.

At Bay's nod, Kyle went to the cabinet and gently opened it to take out the miniature that had distracted him earlier. He took it to Emma.

Looking at him quizzically, she took the miniature and gasped, for there in front of her was a painting of her mom Chione, *but it couldn't be,* she thought, for this painting was centuries of years old.

She looked from the painting to Bay and back to the painting again.

'There is a reason why Amira has always been connected to you Emma. Without you both saving Amira, you wouldn't be here,' said Bay gently.

Emma felt tingles all through her body for the truth was there before her. 'I believe that makes us family,' said Bay. 'I am honoured to welcome you both.'

Emma was overwhelmed by Bay's kindness and the revelation of her ancestry. They hugged and stepped back laughing.

'I need to ring mom and tell her,' said Emma.

'Why don't I show you to the cottage and you can both get settled in and have some privacy. Does dinner at seven o'clock suit you both?' Emma and Kyle both nodded. He led them to the cottage and left them to get settled in. 'Come over when you are ready,' said Bay.

Chapter 49 – Emma and Kyle

'You look beautiful,' declared Chione, her eyes connecting with Emma's in the mirror.

Emma had chosen an Egyptian-style wedding dress with an empire neckline. Gold thread adorned the top of each wide strap around her middle just above her waist. The A-line white lace layered skirt fell gracefully to the floor. Her mom had styled her hair for her so that some of her hair was gathered at the back of her head in a gold and pearl flowered clasp, leaving the rest to fall in waves down her back. White and gold flower clips decorated it throughout, which twinkled in the light when she moved.

There was a knock on the door and her mother-in-law-to-be Jane popped her head in. With a smile, she asked, 'Can I come in?'

'Of course,' said Emma, 'please.'

Smiling at Chione who left saying she would give them a moment, Jane passed Emma a small jewellery box. 'This is from me and Simon.' She indicated for Emma to open the box. Inside the box was a beautiful pair of teardrop earrings. At the top of each was a round green malachite bead, and dangling below this, a clear crystal teardrop.

'They are beautiful, thank you.' And with tears in her eyes, she gave Jane a hug.

'Careful, don't smear your makeup,' she said, and smiling, she passed Emma a tissue. 'I came prepared,' she said.

Chione had outlined Emma's eyes in coal-coloured eyeliner just the way they did in Ancient Egypt and Emma was amazed how exotic her eyes looked. She always thought of her mom's eyes as exotic but never her own. She carefully dabbed at her eyes, careful not to smear her makeup. She fastened each earring and moved her head gently from side to side. 'Perfect,' said Jane, and after another quick hug, she left the room. Chione came in as Jane left with a parcel in her hands. She passed it to Emma.

'This came to me at the museum last month and contained a note to hold it for you until today.'

With shaking hands, Emma opened the parcel. Inside was an ornate jewellery box. Holding her breath, she opened the lid. A part of her suspected what was inside, but she dared not hope. There, nestled in the box, was the amulet. Amira's amulet. There was a note with it that read.

My Dearest Emma,

I know that Amira would like you to wear this on your wedding day. I hope it brings your marriage as many blessings as it did hers.

Yours, Bay

Emma looked at her mom, feeling overwhelmed. Chione nodded her head and smiled. 'Shall I?' Emma nodded her head and Chione took the necklace from the box and fastened it around Emma's neck. It fell perfectly between her breasts and set off her dress and earrings to perfection. 'Now you are ready,' said Chione. Emma picked up the necklace carefully, looking at her reflection in the mirror. Her heart felt full of the love she was surrounded with, and she felt that Amira was right there with her. Her mom slipped out of the room to give her a moment of privacy.

'Thank you, Ami,' Emma said out loud. Letting go of the necklace, she picked up her bouquet, and with one last look at her reflection, she stepped out the room where her dad was waiting to walk her down the aisle.

The opening chords of *From This Moment On* by Shania Twain began to play and Emma took her dad's arm and he started to lead her down the aisle. With the beautiful lyrics to accompany her, Emma made her way towards Kyle, her smile bright and eyes shining.

Kyle watched Emma glide towards him. She was a vision, but what he noticed the most was her radiant and happy smile.

He had eyes only for her. It seemed to take an age and he didn't realise he was holding his breath until her dad passed him her hand and said, 'Breathe,' with a wink.

Then, Emma was standing in front of him. His heart beating in his chest, he took both of her hands in his. 'I love you,' he said, 'you look beautiful.'

'I love you,' said Emma back. That was when he noticed the necklace. He let go of one of her hands and gently picked up the amulet. Releasing it gently, he placed a kiss on Emma's left palm.

'We are truly blessed,' he said. They both turned to the front and the ceremony began.

With close friends and family gathered, they said their vows.

'I now pronounce you husband and wife. You may now kiss the bride.'

As Kyle's lips met Emma's, their first kiss as man and wife, Kyle felt the familiar tingles and dizzy feeling he had felt before. His last thought before the dizziness took over was that he wasn't holding the amulet, but Emma was wearing it. He gripped her hands tightly as the dizzying feeling overwhelmed him.

When he opened his eyes, he was no longer in the church, and to his amazement, Emma was still standing in front of him, her hands clutched tightly in his. 'That was some kiss,' Emma said, before realising that they were no longer in the church. Looking at Kyle with confusion, it finally dawned on her what must have happened, and her mouth formed a perfect oh of shock and awe.

'Did I lose it again?' came a laughing voice behind them. Emma and Kyle swivelled around to see a couple in their late thirties. 'You look beautiful Emma, and very smart Kyle,' said Amira, smiling at them both.

'It's our wedding day,' said Emma.

'Congratulations,' said Amira.

'I can't believe we are here,' said Emma.

'This is Abubakar,' said Amira, introducing the man whose hand she was holding. 'This, my love, is My Truth Seeker Kyle and Emma, My Heart.'

With tears in her eyes, Amira hugged Emma and Kyle shook Abubakar's hand. 'It is nice to finally meet you,' said Abubakar. He had a deep, gentle voice. 'I have much to thank you for.'

Emma and Kyle heard giggles behind them. 'Come, come,' said Amira, taking the hands of two small children. 'They are our grandchildren,' said Amira, introducing the boy and girl who were now looking at Kyle and Emma with interest. 'It is because of you both that they are here. Without you both, they would never have been born. We are both so grateful.'

They talked for a little while longer, trying to exchange as much information as they could. They all knew how brief these meetings could be. 'I suppose it's time that you give that back to me, for the last time I think.'

Reluctantly, Emma took the necklace from around her neck to hand to Amira. 'Thank you for lending it to me to wear at my wedding.'

'How else was I going to see you again?' said Amira mischievously.

'You knew?' said Emma.

Smiling, Amira took the necklace from Emma. 'Goodbye Emma, My Heart. Goodbye Kyle, My Truth Seeker. Be happy and love each other. Oh, and get ready. The next generation is going to bring a new adventure for you both.' Before they could ask her questions, the dizziness began again, and they closed their eyes to prepare. Before they did, Amira blew them both a kiss.

They opened them again to a cheer from the wedding guests and, turning, Kyle led Emma down the aisle to exit the church for photos. Emma's mom Chione kissed her daughter's cheek. 'Congratulation's sweetie.' As Chione released Emma from the embrace, she stopped in mid-step looking at Emma's neck. 'Where is your necklace?' she asked.

Emma's hand came up to her now bare neck, not entirely surprised that the necklace had gone. 'It returned home,' said Emma softly.

Chapter 50 – One Last Gift

It seemed that Amira had one last gift for them.

Upon their return home from their honeymoon, among their post, which Chione had placed on the table along with their wedding gifts, was a parcel.

It was wrapped in brown paper, which is why it stood out from all the brightly wrapped gifts. Written in elegant script on the front was *To the Truth Seeker and My Heart.*

With shining eyes, Emma looked at Kyle and, at his nod, she carefully unwrapped the parcel. She gasped as she looked at what was inside, for bundled together with a silver ribbon were Amira's diaries. Bay had had them bound carefully for them. There was a note with the diaries and Emma passed it to Kyle to read while she undid the ribbon from the diaries and read Amira's words in wonder.

My Dear Emma & Kyle,

I know deep in my heart that Amira would like you both to have these.
I know that they couldn't be in safer hands.

Yours with deep regards
Bay

Emma passed Kyle one of the diaries. 'Do you think she wrote of that night and what happened?' said Kyle.

Emma looked up from the page she was reading. 'She might have.'

'Why don't you have a look? I'll put the kettle on,' said Kyle.

Emma skimmed through the diaries until she found the night in question. Kyle came into the living room with two steaming mugs and set them on the coffee table in front of Emma. 'Did you find anything?' asked Kyle. Emma nodded her head and started to read aloud from Amira's diaries.

I've been having the dream every night for a week. Abubakar has to go away for business, but he is refusing to go.

Strangely, the dreams have stopped. I convinced Abubakar that I would be fine and for him to go, although in my heart I wanted to beg him to stay. He is meeting a new business contact, and they will only deal with him.

He has gone, reluctantly. I promised him I would be fine.

I pray to the gods that I am right.

'The entry stops there. The next entry reads as follows,' said Emma.

I couldn't keep my eyes open any longer, the potion was too strong. I could feel the lone tear track down my cheek. It was then, through the fear, that I realised something. I was still alive. I heard Baahir leave the room and tried to sit up, but it was how I feared, the drug had taken away my ability to move. My mind though, I noticed, was still clear and I could hear. I wasn't sure if this was a blessing or a curse. I wondered if the potion I had made had delayed the effects of the potion. Was I about to hear how I was going to die and not be able to do anything about it? *No*, I told myself, *I must stay calm*. I was still alive and that was a blessing in itself.

I had to believe that Baahir hadn't meant to kill me but to just knock me out. Either that or he hadn't given me enough of the potion to kill me, which was his true intention. I saw that look on his face and remembered what he said before my eyes closed. I had to believe that he didn't want me dead, just out of the way for some purpose. I hoped I was right, and his intention was not to harm me. Either that or the potion I made had counteracted what he gave me. I couldn't be sure, but I needed to stay calm and not let the fear overwhelm me. It was all I had right now.

I heard Baahir come back into the room. He lifted me up and covered me in something. The smell of horse tickled my nose. I could feel him carrying me and then we were outside, I was sure of it. I could feel the cool air and hear muffled birds through whatever he had me wrapped in.

He lay me down and covered me over again with another blanket. I could feel the weight of it. He then left me and the ground around me shifted. No, not ground. He must have me in a cart. I heard the soft nicker of horses and then the harsh sound of a whip against horseflesh, but nothing happened. I heard Baahir cursing, and the ground shifted once more. He was cursing at the horses. I could only assume they didn't want to move. I then felt the cart shift, and someone got in beside me.

A hand gently felt for air below my nose. 'It's Sethos Mrs Isson. Mama sent me,' whispered a voice in my ear. My heart soared at his voice and then fear set in for his safety. I wanted to tell him to run to safety. My mouth was dry, and although I could swallow, and I was obviously still breathing, the drug had taken away my ability to speak or move. I felt comforted that he was there but worried for his safety too. I prayed to the gods that Bay had found his father. I prayed to the gods to protect Sethos for his bravery.

Sethos had hidden himself outside with a clear view of the Isson's home as his mother had instructed. He had seen Baahir leave alone and felt relief. He adjusted his stance in his hiding place to relieve the cramp in his legs but was careful not to make a noise. Unfortunately, Baahir didn't go far. He walked a little way down the Nile and sat on a rock. *What is he doing?* thought Sethos. He crouched back in his hiding place straining to hear for any sign of Baahir's return. It seemed like an age but was probably no time at all. Should he go check on Mrs Isson or wait where he was? He peered out from his hiding place carefully. It was a full moon tonight which helped him see Baahir, but he was also aware he would be just as easily seen. His mama was worried; he had better be cautious. He heard a noise coming from Baahir's direction and saw him make his way back to the Isson's home. *Not leaving then,* he thought. He carefully made his way over to the Isson's home and peered into a window, which had a soft glow coming from it. He could see Mrs Isson lying on the bed and then ducked when Baahir came into view.

He heard his muffled voice as he spoke to Mrs Isson and then he went back out of the room again. Sethos tried to decide whether to call out to Mrs Isson. She was lying so still on the bed. He heard a noise coming from the hallway and quickly slipped around the side of the house.

He peered around the corner carefully but couldn't see anyone. *Should he go back to the window or wait*? he thought. He heard footsteps again and carefully peered around the corner once more. It was Baahir and he was carrying something in his arms wrapped in what looked like a horse blanket. He disappeared down the lane away from the house.

Cautiously, Sethos looked back through the window, but Mrs Isson was gone. He realised that it must have been Mrs Isson that Baahir was carrying. He ran as quietly as he could after Baahir. He saw Baahir climb onto the top of a cart and his heart sank. How was he going to be able to follow on foot? He prayed to the gods for help, and they seemed to answer. Cursing, Baahir got back down off the cart. One of the horses had thrown a shoe and wouldn't move. Making a decision, Sethos took advantage of Baahir's distraction and carefully climbed into the cart and covered himself with the blanket.

The cart jostled as Baahir climbed back on the seat and jolted as the remaining horse was whipped into a trot. Sethos tried to cushion Mrs Isson beside him, as she was jostled by the movement of the cart. The horse gained speed, being whipped to go faster by Baahir. They finally came to a jolting stop and, prepared, Sethos slipped off the back of the cart as quickly as he could and merged into the darkness.

Watching, he saw Baahir carry Mrs Isson to a door and knock. He slipped out of the shadows slightly to see what was happening. Baahir passed his bundle into the arms of a waiting man. 'You know what to do,' he said and turned back towards the cart. Sethos froze in place beside the horse and cart. Seeing him,

Baahir threw him some money. 'Take care of them and they are yours,' he said, walking away, and Sethos sagged with relief.

He looked around him, trying to take in his surroundings. He was outside a funeral home, he realised. He looked at the horse and prayed it had some energy left. Getting into the cart, he shook the reins gently, hoping the horse would be able to take him to Abubakar. He estimated he could reach his ship before daybreak.

The jostling cart finally stopped. I was sure that when feeling came back, if feeling ever came back, that I would be battered and bruised. Sethos had tried to cushion me as much as possible. I would have to thank him later. I heard him slip out of the cart as soon as it came to a halt and prayed that Baahir wouldn't notice him. Baahir knocked on a door and spoke to someone. I then felt myself being taken not too gently from his arms and carried away. 'You know what to do,' he said to whomever held me.

What did that mean, I thought, fearfully? I was placed, none too gently, on a hard surface. 'Careful,' came a voice to my left.

'Why?' came the voice above me and with a snicker, 'she isn't going to feel it.'

'Because she isn't dead,' came the other voice.

'What?'

'I said she isn't dead,' came the voice again. I then felt the covers being pulled away.

'What is she doing here if she isn't dead?' he asked.

'Never mind that, get me that potion. I need to administer it now.'

I felt my mouth being opened and then a few drops of something acidic being dripped onto my tongue which ran down my throat. 'There, just relax, it won't be long,' he said.

'Being kept safe,' said the priest answering the man's question. 'He asked me to help him get her here quietly and to keep her safe.'

'Why?' said the other man. 'Why would you help him? You don't even like him.'

'He did me a favour once,' said the priest. 'He asked me for this in return. If I help him, hopefully I won't ever have to deal with him again.'

'Keeping her safe from who? Or what?' said the other man.

'I don't have to explain myself to you,' said the priest. 'You work for me.

' Grumbling, the other man left the room.

I felt the potion starting to take effect. Pins and needles started to form throughout my body and feeling started to return. 'Why?' I managed through lips still numb.

'I'm so sorry,' said the priest. 'Try to relax. It's not going to be very comfortable as the feeling comes back. You had me worried there; Baahir was much longer than I advised. Rest now. I will bring you some water and try to explain.' So, while the feeling started to return, the priest tried to explain Baahir's plan to me.

Oh Baahir, I thought, *what have you gotten us into and why couldn't you just ask for help.*

Sometime later, I was sitting comfortably, when there was a loud banging at the door. The priest ordered his men to find out who was at the door. 'I suggest you let me in and explain yourself.' It was Abubakar. I could have wept. Abubakar had found me.

Abubakar was worried. He left one of his men behind to keep an eye out for Baahir. At the next few stops, he let a man off to scout around for any news. It wasn't until he had conducted his business that one of his men had news. What he told him made his blood run cold. Baahir had gotten into debt with Abasi who had been overheard threatening to harm Amira and Bennu.

He quickly set sail for home praying he would find Amira safe.

As soon as his ship docked, he grabbed his things. As his feet hit dirt, his son came barrelling towards him from the shadows. 'Slow down,' said Abubakar trying to calm Bay. His son thrust a crumpled piece of paper at him. 'It's Mama,' he said trying to catch his breath.

He quickly scanned the letter from Amira and his worry deepened. Would she still be at home, or would Baahir have taken her somewhere?

He decided to head for home. He called to his ship and one of his men appeared. 'Bay, stay on the ship, I will find your mama, I promise.' Bay tried to protest and Abubakar knelt in front of him. 'You did your mama proud Bay, and so did you Lateef. Stay here, I will bring your mama to you Bay.' He gave him a quick hug and, after making sure that he was safely with one of his men, he started to run for home.

He took some of the back streets trying to shave some time off his journey. As he cut across a street, he heard a horse galloping towards him. He lifted his arms for protection as the horse was halted just in time. 'Mr Isson? Mr Isson, thank the gods. I know where she is sir. I know where Mrs Isson is,' shouted a voice from above. Abubakar recognised the voice as being Sethos, his neighbour's son.

He quickly got on the cart and, taking the reins from the brave Sethos, he turned the cart on the narrow street. Sethos gave him directions to the funeral home and Abubakar prayed that he would reach Amira in time."

Epilogue

Emma walked past Amy's bedroom taking the washing to the kitchen. Amy was playing and chattering away. Emma poked her head in, watching her sharing her book with her teddy and doll to her left and a vacant space to her right.

'Are you having fun sweetie?' Emma said. After a moment, Amy looked up from her book.

'Yes Mommy. Can Cassia stay for tea Mommy?'

'Of course, sweetie? Would Cassia like cake too?'

Amy chatted away and then, with a smile on her face, she nodded at her mom. 'Her favourite is chocolate,' said Amy.

'Ok sweetie, I will be right back.' Smiling to herself, she carried the washing to the kitchen. *That's lucky*, she thought, *as that's Amy's favourite flavour too.*

Kyle was at the kitchen table helping their son Joe with his maths homework. He looked over the top of his glasses at her and wiggled his eyebrows making her giggle. Joe looked up and, rolling his eyes, went back to his homework. 'What were you smiling about when you came into the kitchen?'

'Amy wants her friend to stay for tea and her favourite cake is chocolate just like Amy, fancy that.' Emma said smiling again.

Kyle looked confused. 'What friend? I don't remember anyone coming over, I thought she was playing in her room.'

'She is,' said Emma cryptically. She got two small pieces of cake knowing that Amy would be eating both and walked back upstairs. Kyle was hot on her heels taking two steps at a time, sensing mischief in the air. She indicated for him to be quiet and walked into Amy's bedroom where she was still sitting on the floor. She had gotten out her tea service so that she could serve tea with the cake. Smiling, Emma knelt and placed one plate in front of Amy and one in front of the space to her right which had a teacup waiting. 'One for you,' she said, 'one for Cassia.'

'Thank you, Mommy.' And after looking to her right and nodding, she said, 'Cassia says thank you too. She said it looks yummy.'

'Enjoy,' said Emma, standing up and walking over to Kyle standing in the doorway. He lifted his arm for a hug, and she leant into his side with a contented sigh.

They stood there for about fifteen minutes watching their daughter eat her cake and chat away to her friend, who they couldn't see. They quietly left the room and when they were out of earshot, Kyle turned Emma to face him and with a deadpan voice said. 'So let me get this straight. Our daughter is taking tea with her friend Cassia, who we can't see.' Emma nodded, waiting for the inevitable question. 'And what language exactly was she speaking?'

'It sounded like a mix of Greek and Latin if I'm not mistaken,' said Emma, tilting her head to the side. 'I'm sensing we have some research to do and an adventure to prepare her for.'

The End

The author

Lisa West was born in Northampton in 1975, and now lives in Coventry, England with her husband. Her interests and hobbies include painting and various types of arts and crafts. She also has special skills as a Reiki master and in using crystal therapy. The Truth Seeker, The Seer & The Heart is her first book.